"I don't want to fall

The shock of her words knocked him back half a step. He ran a hand across the back of his neck. "I don't know how to answer that. And besides, I don't think you're in much danger. According to someone I know, I'm bossy and uptight and judgmental and I have a king complex."

"Don't forget arrogant."

He held out his hands. "See? You have nothing to worry about."

They continued walking, but his mind was not on the magnificent scenery. Had Zoe been expecting some sort of reciprocal response on his part after she made her veiled statement about having feelings for him? Had he hurt her by remaining silent? And did he want her to love him? Did he want to love her?

* * *

A Not-So-Innocent Seduction is part of
The Kavanaghs of Silver Glen series:

In the mountains of North Carolina, one family
discovers that wealth means nothing without love

* * *

If you're on Twitter,
tell us what you think of Harlequin Desire!
#harlequindesire

Dear Reader,

It is very exciting to be starting a brand-new family saga here at Harlequin Desire. Already, the Kavanagh men—and the women they love—are weaving their way into my heartstrings. As I get to know them and share their stories with each of you, I hope they will become friends who linger in your memories long after the book is done.

Liam is a character I understand. As a first child myself, I know that being *too* conscientious is not always a good thing. Life should always have room for spontaneity and fun. Zoe helps him stop and smell the roses. But even so, she craves the stability he offers...and the love.

As you find your way around the town of Silver Glen, stop for a donut and a cup of coffee, sit and watch the mountains, revel in the peace of this special valley and its people.

Thanks for joining me on a new journey!

God bless,

Janice Maynard

A NOT-SO-INNOCENT SEDUCTION

JANICE MAYNARD

HARLEQUIN® DESIRE

Recycling programs
for this product may
not exist in your area.

ISBN-13: 978-0-373-73309-5

A NOT-SO-INNOCENT SEDUCTION

Copyright © 2014 by Janice Maynard

Printed in U.S.A.

www.Harlequin.com

Books by Janice Maynard

Harlequin Desire

The Billionaire's Borrowed Baby #2109
*Into His Private Domain #2135
*A Touch of Persuasion #2146
*Impossible to Resist #2164
*The Maid's Daughter #2182
*All Grown Up #2206
*Taming the Lone Wolff #2236
*A Wolff at Heart #2260
A Billionaire for Christmas #2271
Beneath the Stetson #2276
**A Not-So-Innocent Seduction #2296

Silhouette Desire

The Secret Child & the Cowboy CEO #2040

*The Men of Wolff Mountain
**The Kavanaghs of Silver Glen

Other titles by this author available in ebook format.

JANICE MAYNARD

is a *USA TODAY* bestselling author who lives in beautiful east Tennessee with her husband. She holds a B.A. from Emory and Henry College and an M.A. from East Tennessee State University. In 2002 Janice left a fifteen-year career as an elementary school teacher to pursue writing full-time. Now her first love is creating sexy, character-driven, contemporary romance stories.

Janice loves to travel and enjoys using those experiences as settings for books. Hearing from readers is one of the best perks of the job! Visit her website, www.janicemaynard.com, and follow her on Facebook and Twitter.

For Charles—my husband, my best friend. I could dedicate every book to you and never run out of reasons why. Thanks for being my hero. :)

One

Zoe Chamberlain's vintage Volkswagen van, aqua and white with yellow daisies stenciled on the doors, rolled to a halt in the scenic vista pull-off and gave up the ghost. She wasn't too surprised. The engine had been rebuilt three times. But like knowing an aging pet was living on borrowed time, it was hard to imagine letting go.

More than anything or anyone else, Bessie—Zoe's VW bus—was the constant in a life that rarely stayed the same from one week to the next. Apparently, Bessie had decided that Silver Glen, North Carolina, was Zoe's next stop.

Zoe stepped out of the van, yawning and stretching, enjoying the cool morning air and the April sunshine. At her feet, spread out in a narrow valley between two mountainsides, lay a charming town. From this distance the houses and businesses looked like an alpine postcard. Switzerland in miniature.

Unfortunately, the quaint village did not have taxi service. As she scrolled through the options on her phone's search function, she grimaced. Her only choice for transportation appeared to be the Silver Beeches Lodge, a pricey hotel that offered shuttle service. Presumably, they had in mind trips back and forth to the nearest airport, but Zoe had no doubts about her ability to wrangle a ride.

A nomadic lifestyle meant getting along with all sorts of people in all manner of places. Zoe could blarney with the best of them. And she'd been told that her smile could melt the hardest of curmudgeons.

So here she was again. A new town. A new set of problems to handle. In her heart of hearts she knew this couldn't go on much longer. She was tired of running. And her recent illness had taken more out of her than she first realized. The excitement of seeing new horizons every week—sometimes every morning—was beginning to pall. Though she tried to ignore it, a feeling of yearning grew ever stronger. Yearning to put down roots, to feel a part of something bigger than she was.

She had used a quest for adventure as justification for her cowardice. Yes, she had seen the world. And yes, travel was broadening. But the truth was, her past was going to catch up with her. If not here, then in the next place.

It was time to face her demons and take a stand, but she wasn't ready yet. First, she needed rest and time to recoup. Making such a change would be scary.

The town below seemed incredibly peaceful. At this moment in her life, peace was a commodity to be craved. Maybe Silver Glen could offer her that. First on the agenda would be leisure and complete recovery. Once she was back on her feet, both in mind and body, she'd be ready for whatever happened. Hopefully.

She patted Bessie's fender and sighed. "Well, old girl. I guess this is where I'm hanging my hat for a little while. I'll get you towed as soon as I can. In the meantime, enjoy the view."

Liam Kavanagh spotted the slender blonde the moment she set foot in the lobby. She would be hard to miss under any circumstances, but carrying a guitar case and wearing a multicolored cotton skirt that swished around her ankles, she looked like a 1960s love child returning from an outdoor rock concert. The bounce in her step and the upward curve of her lips gave her a girl-next-door appeal.

The highly trained staff at the Silver Beeches knew to greet guests with warmth and charm. Liam had watched them in action time and again. He rarely took the time to personally interact with visitors unless they were close friends of his.

He didn't know this woman. At all. But some powerful response propelled his feet forward. Before Pierre, the concierge, could offer to help, Liam intercepted the eye-catching female. "Welcome to the Silver Beeches Lodge. May I help you?"

The woman hitched a large raffia tote higher on her shoulder and gave him a winsome smile. Her eyes were the blue of a summer sky. "I'd like to check in, please."

He lifted a mental eyebrow. Rooms in the hotel started at eight hundred a night and went up from there. This beautiful creature hardly seemed the type to avail herself of the upscale amenities, but he'd been surprised before. "Do you have a reservation?" he asked.

"I do. Made it online an hour ago. Is that a problem?"

He deserved her frown. The tone of his voice had come across as suspicious. He shrugged. "Of course not. I thought I had looked at all of today's check-ins, but I must have missed yours since it was recent. Welcome." He motioned for her to accompany him. "Marjorie, there at the desk, will take care of you. Please let me know if you need anything at all. Our wish is to make you as comfortable as possible."

"So gallant," she said, smiling at him in a way that made the back of his neck hot.

Was she mocking him? It wouldn't be the first time someone had accused him of being too serious. "It's what we do," he said, wincing at the stiffness he heard in his response. He didn't intend to be a stuffed shirt, but he'd been the head of a large and rowdy family since his father disappeared over two decades ago. The weight of his responsibility—and a certain bitterness about his father's lack thereof—didn't leave much room for lightheartedness.

He nodded briefly and excused himself as Marjorie took over. Crossing the lobby to where Pierre held court, he kept an eye on the newcomer. "Not our usual clientele."

Pierre pursed his lips. In his sixties now, he had worked for the Kavanagh family since he was a young man. He wore his formal black tuxedo with pride and ruled his realm with a firm hand. "Pretty," he said.

Liam nodded absently. He couldn't place her age. Pale skin so pure and fine it seemed almost translucent made her seem youthful, but in her serene gaze he saw the patina of experience. He wasn't sure why she fascinated him so. Perhaps because she was the antithesis of the expertly made-up women who often checked into the Lodge.

Visitors to the Silver Beeches were either retirees with plenty of disposable income, younger generations whose careers afforded them fame and fortune, or merely those who wanted to hide from the world. Privacy was an unspoken amenity. From rock stars to movie idols, from politicians to European royalty, every guest was pampered.

As a bellman came in from outside with the new guest's single suitcase, Marjorie handed a key card to the young woman and pointed her toward the elevators. When the bellman and his charge disappeared, Marjorie slipped from behind the desk and approached Liam and Pierre.

Liam frowned slightly. "Problem?"

Marjorie, a stout woman in her mid-fifties with salt-and-pepper hair, shook her head. "Not exactly. But I thought you'd want to know. She booked a basic room for six weeks."

Both men stared at her. Liam recovered first, though his gut tightened with unease. "Any problem with authorizing her method of payment?"

The seasoned receptionist shook her head. "Platinum card. No limit. But tell me—who books a reservation like that on the day of arrival? Spontaneity is one thing, but this is weird, don't you think?"

Liam kept his expression neutral with effort. Red flags were popping up all over the place, but he didn't want his staff to see that he was perturbed. "I'm sure she has her reasons."

Pierre straightened his spine, his gaze fierce. "I'll keep an eye on her, sir. If there's any funny business, I'll let you know."

Maeve Kavanagh appeared from the direction of the back stairs, her bun slightly askew and her reading glasses dangling from a chain around her neck. Liam's mother was a vibrant sixty-year-old with dark snapping eyes and a nose for sniffing out trouble. "You all three look like you've eaten a lemon. What's going on?"

Liam kissed her on the cheek. "Not a thing. Marjorie checked in a new guest. We were merely speculating about her background."

Maeve sniffed. "Not your place," she said firmly. "You know I can't abide gossip."

Liam smiled wryly. "Yes, ma'am. I remember." Inwardly, he was far less amused. The irregularities about the new guest's booking set his teeth on edge. He hated mysteries and secrets. His father's hidden life had nearly destroyed their family. And in the end had led to Reggie Kavanagh's premature death.

The one trait Liam couldn't abide in a woman, or a man for that matter, was a predilection to bend the truth. Even if the potential prevaricator came wrapped in a very appealing package.

Before he could give in to the temptation to initiate further contact with the blonde, he managed a smile for his mother and Pierre and Marjorie. "If you three will excuse me, I have some calls to make." Striding down the hall to his office, he told himself he was jumping to conclusions.

The newcomer could have any number of valid reasons for deciding on the spur of the moment to stay alone at a pricey hotel for six weeks.

Trouble was, despite his best efforts, Liam couldn't come up with a single one.

Zoe grilled the bellman on the way upstairs. "So tell me. Who's the yummy guy that looks like a young Harrison Ford?"

The teenage bellhop grinned. "That's Mr. Kavanagh. Mr. Liam Kavanagh. His family owns the Silver Beeches. Well, that and most of the town, as well."

"He works for a living?" She was surprised. In her experience, the überrich kept to themselves as much as possible.

The young man waited politely for her to step out of the elevator when they reached the top floor. "Every one of the Kavanagh men does something. They were brought up to respect a hard day's work, even though the whole family is richer than God. Mr. Liam manages the hotel along with his mother."

Inside the room, Zoe reached in her bag for a generous tip that made the kid's eyes light up. "Thanks for your help," she said.

He bowed awkwardly. "All you have to do is dial the front desk if you need anything. Room service is available 24/7. In the center drawer of the dresser you'll find listings about all the restaurants here and off-site as well. Welcome to Silver Glen."

Alone in her luxurious new quarters, Zoe opened the armoire and smiled as she imagined how little of the space her belongings would fill. Learning to travel light had been a necessary lesson, and one she had mastered long ago. Nevertheless, she carefully unloaded her suitcase and put away everything she had brought with her. Being neat was perhaps a relic of her parents' influence, the one trait she couldn't shake.

There were still a few items in the van, but nothing she

needed urgently. She turned in a slow circle, taking in every detail of her new accommodations. Here in the mountains of North Carolina, one might have expected a more rustic decor, but the Silver Beeches Lodge was elegant in the extreme.

The lobby alone telegraphed that message. Italian marble floors. Sparkling chandeliers. Priceless Oriental rugs of massive size. Enormous urns filled with fresh flowers. It had taken Zoe only moments to decide that Bessie had been correct about her silent suggestion. Zoe needed to rest, and this lovely hotel promised to be peaceful.

Never mind that it cost an arm and a leg. Her usual lifestyle was lean and frugal, so this splurge would not break the bank. Besides, after the winter she had endured, she deserved a little pampering.

Walking barefoot across the plush ivory carpet, she opened her guitar case and removed the instrument. The comfy bay-window seat was covered in crimson velvet. Poor Bessie would never have made it up the incline to the hotel. The Silver Beeches Lodge had literally been built into the side of the mountaintop, and its location gave guests a bird's-eye view of the valley floor far below.

Zoe curled her legs beneath her and bent her head over the instrument that had traveled so many miles with her. Strumming it absently, she hummed a tune that had been dancing in her head. She'd had to resist the urge to coax the bellhop into lingering for a bit to answer her questions about the hotel owner. Just because she was lonely was no reason to get the kid in trouble.

Her reaction to meeting Liam Kavanagh was the equivalent of experiencing a crush on a movie star. His in-your-face masculinity made her feel dainty and feminine. She might even have swooned a little bit. Even now, her throat flushed as she remembered the way he looked at her. The man was a walking fantasy. She glanced out the window and sighed.

Night was falling rapidly, and shadows crept across the

valley. Her stomach rumbled. She remembered that her last meal had been an orange and a Diet Coke at a rest stop on I-40. She wished she could go into town and explore, but until Bessie was fixed, she was stuck here in the hotel. Dialing room service, she ordered a large dinner, including a serving of tiramisu. She was still a good fifteen pounds underweight, so the extra calories wouldn't hurt her.

She'd spent the last week in Asheville playing at a little coffee shop in the downtown district. Asheville was filled with artists and performers and had a character and charm that delighted her. If she'd had her way, she might have bought a place and put down some roots. But one evening she had seen a familiar face on the street, and she had known it was time to move on. The hotel's strict privacy policy would stand her in good stead. No one would know she was here, and if she wore a bit of a disguise in town, she might be able to stay for even longer than the month and a half she had booked.

After finishing her larger-than-normal meal, she felt both satiated and guilty. Changing into yoga pants and a sports bra, she checked the hotel directory and discovered that the workout facility was located on the basement level. She threw a light jacket over her shoulders, more for modesty than anything else, grabbed her room key and a bottle of water, and slipped out the door.

Liam strained with all his might as he lifted the challenging weights in one last rep. Red-faced and sweating, he wiped his forehead and neck with a towel, realizing ruefully that the punishing exercise had not dulled the throbbing arousal that plagued him.

He wasn't sporting an erection, but his body hummed with the need for sex. It had been too long, and the blonde who checked in that afternoon was exactly the type he found irresistible. Her silky hair brushed her shoulder blades. Though she was thin, her curves were all woman.

If she was staying for an entire six weeks, he would have to be on his guard. Just because he felt a visceral interest in Ms. Zoe Chamberlain didn't mean the feelings were reciprocated. And because there was clearly more to Zoe than met the eye, he wouldn't allow himself to pursue the attraction. Most men were vulnerable to a sexy woman. But Liam understood the consequences of becoming entangled with a liar.

If he had to choose between satisfying the burning in his gut and being won over by a con, he would take a lot of cold showers. Zoe's seeming innocence was dangerous. He'd learned the hard way at age sixteen that a pretty face could disguise a multitude of sins. He would cut off his hand before he ever put his mother and siblings through that kind of pain again. As the head of the Kavanaghs, his loyalty to his family superseded any fleeting attraction he might experience.

Besides, for all he knew, Zoe could be married. He couldn't imagine any husband in his right mind letting such a fresh, appealing woman take a solo six-week vacation, but who knows? The Silver Beeches had seen more than its share of odd relationships over the years.

After showering and changing back into his dress shirt and slacks, he wandered out into the gym only to stop dead when he saw his new guest walking briskly on a treadmill. Her slender frame resonated with life and passion. At the moment, she was the only occupant of the facility other than himself, and he didn't want to startle her. She was wearing earbuds attached to an iPod tucked into a hot-pink armband. Her ponytail swung energetically in time to the music only she could hear.

Despite his lofty intentions and self-lecturing, he was drawn to her as inexorably as a green boy seeing his first seminude woman. His heartbeat picked up even as his breathing grew choppy. Telltale signs that his libido was far more powerful than his intellect.

Deciding to take the long way around to the door, Liam

assumed she would see him in her peripheral vision and thus not be alarmed. But even though he stayed far to the other side of the room, as soon as she caught sight of him, she hopped off the treadmill, shut it down and removed her earphones. "Hello, Mr. Kavanagh."

As she walked toward him, he studied the sensual grace in her movements. "You know who I am?" Though he tried to keep his gaze on her face, only a saint could ignore the rest of her body. Her Lycra-covered curves were mesmerizing…. That and the sheen of perspiration on her skin. He imagined she would look just this way after an enthusiastic round of lovemaking.

She nodded, wiping her forehead with her forearm. "I pumped the bellman for details about you. A failing of mine. Curiosity killed the cat, and all that."

Liam liked knowing she was interested enough to ask questions. That was a good sign if he planned on pursuing her. Which he wouldn't. Probably. He ran a hand through his hair, knowing from her expression that she had recognized his sexual interest. "A fairly minor sin, I'd say. Are you satisfied with your room?"

She lifted an eyebrow. "Are you kidding? It's amazing. The view alone is worth the price. Your hotel is beautiful."

"Thank you. My family built it just after World War II. And we've continued to add on and make improvements as the years go by." He'd never had any trouble talking to women, but for some reason he didn't understand, Zoe made his palms sweat. She wasn't the most beautiful woman he'd ever met, nor the most polished. Usually, people were intimidated by *him,* not vice versa. He couldn't say why he was bungling what should have been a casual, polite encounter, but he was sure she didn't want to hear a documentary on the Silver Beeches. "I'd better get back upstairs."

She cocked her head. "Was your offer sincere?"

"I beg your pardon?" Her artless question befuddled him. "You said you would do anything to make me comfortable. I'm merely asking if that was standard hotel hyperbole, or if you meant it."

He felt his neck get warm. Was she coming on to him, or was she merely eccentric? "Of course, I meant it. Was there something you wanted?"

Zoe supposed it would be poor form to blurt out *You!* Even if his intensity and unsmiling sexiness definitely flipped her switches. She was having a hard time reading Liam Kavanagh. He seemed interested in her the way a man is interested in a woman he wants, but on the other hand, his body language telegraphed a definite wariness. Maybe he felt like she was too bourgeois to stay at his fancy hotel.

If that were the case, she wouldn't disabuse him. She was a pro at keeping secrets. Perhaps Liam might have a few of his own. Could two people with such defenses in place make any kind of connection?

Her walkabout ways the last few years had made it virtually impossible to sustain any kind of deep relationship with a man. Since she wasn't into casual hookups, she ended up alone most of the nights of her life. Ordinarily, she was able to convince herself that solitude was preferable to intimacy with a guy who might turn out to be a jerk.

But now, with Liam Kavanagh in touching distance, she was suddenly and intensely aware of how long it had been since she'd been with a man. She was young and healthy. Liam exuded all sorts of breath-stealing pheromones. She had a gut feeling that his experience was exponentially ahead of hers…and that he was the kind of man a woman never forgot.

What frightened her was the knowledge that he was unlike any man she had ever wanted before. Was her whole life about to change? She'd been prepared to face her mistakes. But Liam was a bend in the road she hadn't anticipated. Could she deal with the complicated past and the intriguing present all at once? He didn't appear to be a man who would be easily *handled.*

Clearing her throat, she summoned a cheeky smile. Liam's wary courtesy made her want to ruffle his feathers. "I've never been to Silver Glen before," she said. "How about buying me a drink in the bar and giving me a quick rundown of the *must-sees.*" She knew how to flirt. It came naturally to her upbeat personality despite the fact that she lived like a nun most of the time.

He appeared taken aback by her request. But he recovered rapidly, his gaze scanning her from head to toe with an assessment that was as personal as her deliberate come-on. "I could do that."

A nasty thought occurred to her. "I suppose I should ask. Is there a Mrs. Kavanagh?"

He nodded, sending her heart to her knees. "Yes. My mother. But she goes to bed early, so I doubt she'd want to join us."

"So you *do* have a sense of humor," she taunted, refusing to admit—even to herself—that she was elated by the confirmation that he was single. Not all married men wore wedding rings, so she hadn't been sure. "I was beginning to think they removed your funny bone at birth."

His lips twitched. "I'm guessing you weren't spanked enough as a kid."

"And there you'd be wrong," she said, her stomach twisting involuntarily. "Let me shower and I'll join you in the lobby in half an hour. Does that work for you?"

He nodded slowly, regarding her with watchful eyes that were a brilliant, intense blue. Combined with his thick, coal-black hair, she began to see the Irish ancestry his name suggested.

She'd provoked him, and now he regarded her with a narrow-eyed gaze. "I'll be there, Ms. Chamberlain. And I'll have the kitchen deliver some special hors d'oeuvres to the bar."

"I've already had dinner," she felt compelled to point out.

"You'll enjoy these," he promised. "Nothing too heavy."

"Does every guest get this personal treatment?"

Now, there was no mistaking his interest. "Only the ones who ask," he said, the words calm and crisp. "I'll see you shortly."

Zoe decided not to shower in the dressing room. She hadn't brought clean clothes with her, so it was easier to dart back up to her room and use the sumptuous facilities that made her feel decadent and a bit naughty. The clothes she'd had on earlier were somewhat travel-weary, so she reached in the armoire for a slinky black knit dress that packed like a dream. It showed every curve of her body, but she had worn it enough times to feel at ease in the sexy garment. Most of a woman's appearance was dictated by confidence. Since she had learned stage presence long ago, it was easy to project an image, even if she didn't feel her best inside.

Timidity and nerves could be disguised. In some of her darker moments—when faced with a bully or an amorous drunk who didn't want to back off—she'd learned that the only way to prevail was to act like she didn't give a damn. How many times over the years had she done exactly that? Liam was no doubt a perfectly lovely man, but the ability to appear comfortable when she was uncertain of an outcome would stand her in good stead.

Shaking off the dark memories, she inserted small gold studs in her earlobes and slipped her feet into black patent high-heeled sandals. The sleeveless dress was fairly modest except for the fact that it hugged her body. She glanced in the mirror and sighed. How long had it been since she shared an elegant meal with a man?

Most of the time, she was the music in the background of someone else's life. She had planned it that way…enjoyed it mostly. But tonight, she looked forward to enjoying Liam

Kavanagh's courtly manners. And perhaps slipping past his facade of propriety.

She spritzed perfume at her ears and wrists and slipped a delicate gold chain around her neck. It hung between her breasts and caught the light. Somewhere, in a safety-deposit box far away, she had a large collection of expensive jewelry...pearls, diamonds, semiprecious stones. But as long as she played the role of gypsy, her baubles would go unclaimed. She didn't care. Not really. But tonight it would have been nice to gild the lily with a bit of sparkly, feminine bling.

Taking a deep breath, she tucked her room key and phone into a small bag and headed for the door. Liam Kavanagh was downstairs, and she didn't intend to keep him waiting.

Two

Liam bobbled his glass of wine—splashing a few drops on his hand—when Zoe walked into the bar. All heads swung in her direction, though she appeared oblivious to the interest she drew. Finally, he pinpointed part of her allure. It was the way she moved…graceful, energetic, as if she were always off on a delightful adventure.

Liam had been standing by the bar talking to the female bartender. With a lift of his hand, he caught Zoe's attention, hoping his smile appeared more natural than it felt. His limbs tingled and his chest tightened. The physical manifestations of his arousal were disconcerting. He'd had a number of lovers in his adult life. He understood sexual hunger. But the intensity of his response to Zoe rattled him.

The dress she wore should have been outlawed. Even the harshest of critics would have to concede that it was modest in cut. A shallow scooped neck front and back, plus a hemline that covered her ankles, might have added up to a demure appearance. But the soft, pliable fabric slid over Zoe's phenomenal body like a second skin.

He spent a good thirty seconds searching for any evidence that she wore underwear.

"Hello, Liam," she said, her voice smooth as cream. "May I call you that?"

He took her hand and lifted it to his lips. "I think you just did."

Chuckling softly, she allowed him to seat her at a table for two tucked away in a shadowy corner. The bar was crowded tonight. He was glad. The public setting gave him time to get to know her and to decide if she was any kind of threat. Kissing her later seemed a foregone conclusion, but he would at least pretend to himself that he had a choice.

She glanced around the room. "Nice place. You and your family have good taste."

"Thank you. I'm assuming you won't be offended if I use your first name as well?"

"Of course not."

"We've only just met. Some people prefer a bit of formality."

"Not me. Social conventions get in the way."

"In the way of what?"

She shrugged. "I don't know. Becoming friends, I suppose."

He took a sip of his wine, trying to read the subtext, if there was any. Before he could reply, a waiter appeared and set a plate of appetizers in front of them. Small wedges of melon and scallops wrapped in prosciutto had been skewered with toothpicks. He selected one and held it out. "Our chef is spectacular. Try a bite."

He'd anticipated an argument. Instead, her lips parted and she leaned forward, allowing him to slide the delicacy between her lush, glossy, pale-pink lips. "Wonderful," she said, after she chewed and swallowed. "Thank you."

The sensuality and simple enjoyment in her response made him shift restlessly in his chair. As she sat back and smiled at him, her wavy golden hair swung around her shoulders. He couldn't decide if she was trying to be provocative, or if he was overly sensitive to her allure.

At that moment, his mother appeared at his shoulder. "Hope I'm not interrupting. Please introduce me to this lovely girl," she said.

A waiter scurried over with a third chair, and Liam stood until his mother was seated. Maeve Kavanagh had never been able to resist poking her nose into Liam's affairs, either literal or metaphorical ones. Because he loved her dearly, he tolerated her interference, particularly since he hoped to get her impressions of the mysterious blonde. "Zoe Chamberlain, meet Maeve Kavanagh, my mother."

The two women shook hands. Zoe grinned wryly. "I'm happy to meet you. But you're far too young to be Liam's mother. I think he gave me the wrong impression when he described you." She crossed her legs beneath the table, the toe of her shoe brushing the crease in his trouser leg. Was she doing that on purpose?

Maeve shot him a glance that made the tops of his ears heat. "My firstborn has an odd sense of humor at times. We make allowances for him." She helped herself to an appetizer. "What brings you to Silver Glen, Ms. Chamberlain? Business or vacation?"

"Call me Zoe, please. And actually, it's neither. I had a nasty bout of pneumonia back in March. Spent a few days in the hospital. Since then I've been taking things easy. Your beautiful hotel seemed like the perfect place to rest and regain my stamina."

"You've come to the right spot. We'll pamper you so well you won't want to go home."

Serious illness explained her fragile appearance. Which led Liam to more questions. He inserted himself into the conversation. "And on that note, where *is* home, Zoe?"

For the first time, he saw her good humor waver. A shadow crossed her expressive face. But she recovered quickly. "I was born in Connecticut, but I haven't lived there in years."

"That's not really an answer."

Her jaw tightened. "Am I being interrogated?"

Maeve Kavanagh's phone buzzed, signaling the arrival of a text. She glanced at it and grimaced. "Duty calls." She stood and patted Liam's shoulder. "Try not to alienate our newest guest, son. I'd like her to stay for a while."

In the silence that followed his mother's departure, Liam stared moodily at his tablemate. "Since when is polite conversation categorized as interrogation?"

She shrugged. "So far, the conversation has been pretty one-sided. I'm picking up weird vibes from you. Is there a problem you want to talk about?"

"No." *Yes.* "Feel free to cross-examine me if it will make you feel better. My family is an open book. Ask anyone in town. They'll tell you."

"There's no such thing as a clan without skeletons in the closet. But I'll take you at your word. Do you have siblings?"

"More than I care to count. It's the Irish Catholic thing. My mother deserves sainthood."

"And your father?"

He couldn't help the wave of anger that made his entire body go rigid. "He died when I was sixteen."

"I'm sorry." Her response was quiet. In her steady gaze he saw recognition of his turmoil. But he didn't want anyone psychoanalyzing him. He ate another appetizer, his gaze drifting over the noisy but genteel crowd. "It was a long time ago," he muttered, and was relieved when she allowed the subject to drop.

"Did you always know you wanted to run the hotel?"

"No. In fact, I had dreams of becoming a major-league football player."

Her jaw dropped and she laughed out loud.

He scowled. "What's so funny?"

You don't really seem the type."

"I can assure you, Zoe, I've played more than my share of high school and college sports."

"I wasn't impugning your athletic ability or your masculinity. It's just that you seem rather sophisticated for the rough-and-tumble world of professional sports."

"Sophistication is nothing more than clothes and demeanor. After my father's death, it became clear that my studies were headed in a new direction. As soon as I finished an MBA, I returned home to assist my mother."

"Did you really have no choice?" It sounded like more than a rhetorical question.

"No one dragged me back in chains, if that's what you mean. But I felt the obligation of being the oldest. The others were still growing up. It was me or no one."

"I see."

His explanation seemed to bother her, though he couldn't fathom why. "At the risk of sounding nosy, what did *you* study in college?"

"I spent four semesters at Vassar. Decided I had no clue what I wanted to do with my life, so I dropped out and joined the Peace Corps."

"Are you serious?" More and more he got the impression that she was a throwback to the 1960s.

"It was wonderful," she said simply. "And eye-opening. I was young and naive and had no clue that extreme third-world poverty existed."

"Your parents were okay with you leaving school?"

"I didn't really ask them."

The more she revealed, the more he wanted to know. But she had accused him of interrogating her, and he had to respect her boundaries…not only because she was a guest in the hotel, but because it was the right thing to do.

"Would you like another drink?" he asked.

"A peach daiquiri would be nice." Zoe cocked her head. "Why are you entertaining me?"

He summoned a waiter and gave their order. When the young man disappeared, Liam met her gaze squarely. "Has it occurred to you that *you* may be entertaining me?"

For the first time since they met in the lobby, he saw her flustered. Her cheeks flushed a rosy pink and she looked away for a moment. He used the opportunity to study her profile. The only thing marring a classically beautiful face was the thrust of a stubborn chin and the smallest of crooks in her nose.

His scrutiny did not go unnoticed. Her hands fiddled with a fork as she faced him again. "Do I have food on my face?" she asked, the words acerbic.

"Sorry. I was just wondering if you had ever broken your nose."

"That bad, huh?"

"Not at all. But you have the features of a Greek goddess except for that tiny crooked place in your nose and the way you lead with your chin."

"I'm not sure that counts as a compliment."

"Merely trying to avoid social conventions."

Finally, he coaxed a smile from her. "Touché."

Their drinks arrived. Zoe sipped hers delicately, like a small child savoring an unaccustomed treat. He wanted to ask her flat out if she could afford a six-week stay at Silver Beeches, but of course, he couldn't. Attending Vassar indicated a certain level of financial ease. Then again, she could have gone on a scholarship. The fact that he was so obsessed with her background gave him pause. Was his interest related to the hotel, or something more?

A man could want a woman without knowing anything at all about her other than the way she walked and the scent of her perfume. Simple lust he understood. But this fixation on ferreting out Zoe's secrets alarmed him. Whether she was an eccentric heiress or a working girl with only months to live or European royalty hiding out from the press, her story was hers to tell.

Perhaps if he were patient, Zoe would open up to him. Two decades ago he had allowed infatuation to blind him to the truth about a woman. It had been a salutary lesson, and one he wouldn't repeat. The fact that he was already so intrigued by Zoe meant he had to be very careful not to let his hormones overrule his common sense.

Zoe was having the most marvelous time. Dressed up for a change. Chatting with a suave, worldly, handsome man. Feeling like a desirable woman. All in all, quite an exceptional evening.

Liam was fascinating. On the outside, the epitome of a sophisticated gentleman. But in his conversation and in his eyes, she caught glimpses of another man, another less polished persona.

What did it say about her that she wanted to see more of the second?

She savored the last bit of her drink, feeling the pleasant buzz in her limbs as the alcohol worked its way through her bloodstream. She was not much of a drinker and had little tolerance for strong spirits. The daiquiri had just enough of a punch to leave her relaxed and happy.

Liam seemed in no hurry to end their encounter, so she lingered as well, even as the bar emptied slowly. It was fun to pick out the honeymooners, the anniversary couples. A few duos exhibited the marks of enjoying a clandestine affair.

Watching people was a hobby of Zoe's. She knew how to fade into the background, especially with her guitar around her neck.

Over the years, her people skills had carried her far and had kept her out of harm's way. A single woman on the road had to be smart and well prepared. Despite her current slenderness, she knew how to fell an assailant and how to disable an aggressor.

Tonight, however, such skills would not be needed. Liam was not the kind of man who had to force himself on a woman. The intensity of his eyes made her shiver. They were technically the same color as hers. But in Liam's case, the blue was the searing shade found in the heart of a flame.

He had unbuttoned the top button of his shirt and loosened his tie. At the end of a long day, his jaw was shadowed. She imagined for a moment what he would look like in bed, ready for sleep after making love to a woman.

Her thighs tightened and her belly quivered. Perhaps Bessie had been wrong. Perhaps Silver Glen, North Carolina, presented danger rather than a safe haven. Zoe rarely had difficulty guarding her heart. Her transient lifestyle kept relationships at bay.

But then again, she had never met a man like Liam who appealed to her so immediately and so viscerally. Contentment ruled her days for the most part, even if loneliness had to be acknowledged and embraced.

For Liam Kavanagh she was willing to change all that. She knew it in an instant. Perhaps she was even willing to blindly follow the demands of her body and give in to the sweet rush of arousal. Throwing herself into an impulsive affair was completely out of character. But her illness during the late winter had shaken her.

Lying in a strange hospital in Albuquerque, New Mexico, near death at one point, she had hit rock bottom. No one knew where she was. There were no friends nearby to bring flowers and pop in for a visit. If she had slipped away into the great beyond, her passing would have sparked little more interest than a search for next of kin.

Shame and distress made her tremble. She had been on the run for so long that she no longer knew how to relax and enjoy life. She told herself that her needs were few. That traveling light was a virtue. But at the end of the day, what did she have to show for her twenty-seven years on this earth?

Contemplating change was difficult. And terrifying.

Liam reached across the table and took one of her hands in his. "Are you okay, Zoe? You've gone pale as milk. And you're shaking. It's late. If you've been ill, perhaps you need to be in bed."

Was it her imagination, or did his fingers tighten on hers involuntarily when he said the word *bed?*

She managed a smile. "I'm fine. Maybe a ghost walked over my grave."

"Are you superstitious?"

"No more than the next person, I suppose. But the Irish are, I'm told. Though you don't strike me as the type of man who leans toward whimsy or flights of fancy."

He released her. The color of his eyes darkened to midnight. His jaw set. "I've seen firsthand the pain caused by people who can't hold on to reality. So, no. I'm not superstitious."

The turn in the conversation had upset him. But she couldn't let it drop. "And I've seen the damage done by soulless individuals who can't see the magic in everyday life. So maybe the truth lies somewhere in between."

They stared at each other. A pleasant evening of flirtation had segued into something far more serious.

He shook his head, his expression rueful. "I think we've strayed into territory best left unexplored for the moment. I was supposed to be telling you about things to see and do while you're here."

"True." She glanced at his watch. "But it's late. We can finish this tomorrow. I need to get some sleep."

He stood when she did. "I'll walk you to your room."

"It's not necessary."

His gaze was teasing. "Merely one of our amenities."

They exited the bar and headed for the duo of elevators in the lobby. Someone had lowered the lights. A sleepy desk clerk sketched a halfhearted wave as they passed by. The intimacy of the hour shrouded everything in a hushed silence.

In the elevator, Zoe leaned against one mirrored wall, Liam the other. His gaze was trained on the carpet at his feet, as though he were lost in thought. The ride was short. A quiet ding, and suddenly they were at Zoe's floor.

"Good night," she said, thinking he would remain in the elevator.

Instead, he accompanied her down the hallway. "Perhaps I should check for monsters under your bed," he whispered, obviously not wanting to disturb his other guests.

She shot him a look, wondering if he expected to come in. "I'm sure a hotel like the Silver Beeches Lodge has a ghostbuster on retainer. But thanks for the offer."

At her door, she reached in her small bag and withdrew her key card. "I enjoyed our visit," she said primly. "Thanks for your time."

They were not touching. Liam stood a good three feet away. But the look in his eyes scorched her. Beneath the thin fabric of her dress, her nipples beaded.

Liam noticed, and took a step backward. "It was my pleasure," he said. The words were prosaic, but the intonation was not.

Desire shimmered between them, invisible but real. She didn't really imagine that her vehicle talked to her. That was a game she played. But if she believed in fate, and perhaps she did, then this moment in time was preordained. Something had brought her to a small, private getaway in the mountains where the man of her dreams awaited her.

It was entirely possible she was being naive. Perhaps Liam entertained a number of female guests who walked into his hotel.

Even so, she chose to keep the fiction alive.

She looked at him wistfully, wishing she had the guts to kiss him. "Good night, Liam."

He nodded tersely, his beautiful eyes turbulent. "Good night, Zoe."

Three

Liam didn't sleep worth a damn. His sex was stiff and aching off and on for most of the night. The few hours he did manage to close his eyes and doze, he dreamed of Zoe. When the alarm went off at seven, he groaned and slapped the snooze button. Normally a morning person, today he knew it was going to take more than a cup of coffee—or two or four—to keep him on track.

The dreams he'd experienced had been explicit and erotic. In his extremely vivid nocturnal imagination, Zoe was continually naked and smiling. And happy to see him. He could actually feel the warmth of her body draped across his. A pleasant notion that played well in his subconscious, but not so much in the harsh light of day.

The alarm shrilled a second time, and he gave in.

An hour later, showered, dressed and mostly awake, he headed down to the lobby. It was a weekday, so their check-ins would be light. Marjorie stopped him with a question about a multiroom booking. Pierre wanted to show him a website that might be of interest to their guests. By the time Liam finally made it to his office, it was almost ten.

He sat down at his desk and opened his laptop, gazing absently out his window that overlooked the side of the property. The groundskeeper had outdone himself this past year. Dogwoods bloomed in profusion amidst carefully sculpted banks of forsythia. Narrow paths dotted with ornamental benches invited guests to stop and enjoy the rainbow of irises, tulips and English wildflowers planted in traditional beds.

The tranquil view soothed Liam as a rule. But today it made things worse. Because he could imagine himself and Zoe walking in the moonlight out there. A glance at the calendar on the wall confirmed the fact that the lunar phase was full tonight.

Sucking in a disgusted breath, he forced himself to focus on work. He was a grown man too old to be ruled by his male anatomy. Last night was exhilarating and stimulating in more ways than one. But he had to slow down. He was the head of the Kavanagh family. He had responsibilities. Big ones. He didn't have the luxury of following every sexual whim.

The landline phone rang, startling him. He picked it up automatically. "Silver Beeches Lodge. Liam Kavanagh speaking."

The voice on the other end was familiar. "Hey, buddy. Do you have a minute to come down to the shop?"

"What's up, Gary?" He and the owner of the Silver Chassis had gone to public school together for years and remained friends to this day, despite the differences in their financial situations. Maeve had taught her children from the cradle that they were no better than anyone else. *Money is not the measure of a man.* Liam had heard those words from her a hundred times.

Silver Glen's most talented mechanic lowered his voice. "I don't want to say anything over the phone. But I think you'll want to see this."

Liam snagged a bagel and a banana from the hotel kitchen and ate them on the way down the mountain. The scenic drive was so familiar, he could have done it in his sleep, but the view affected him every time. This town would not exist without Kavanagh ancestors. Every part of the community had Kavanagh blood running through its veins.

For Liam it was both a blessing and a curse. He was proud to be a part of something so special, but he was ruefully aware that his heritage chained him here as certainly as any prison bars.

He'd taken up the yoke after his father's disappearance. He had stood beside his grieving mother and sworn to keep their family together and afloat. But in the process, he'd given up any autonomy over his future. The road ahead was never going to change. He had trained himself to ignore the bleak disappointment that knowledge occasionally evoked.

He parked on the street behind Gary's shop and went in search of the owner. Gary was in the pit, examining the undercarriage of a vintage VW bus. When he noticed Liam's presence, he called out. "Hold on." Moments later, he climbed up and joined Liam. "This is what I wanted to show you."

Liam frowned. "I don't understand."

Gary was balding prematurely and had a bit of a beer gut, but he knew cars better than anyone Liam had ever met. "It was towed here this morning by an automobile service. The owner contacted me and gave me carte blanche to replace the engine and anything else that needed attention."

"So?"

"So," Gary said with a grimace, "the owner has checked into your hotel."

Liam shook his head in disbelief as the light dawned. "Zoe Chamberlain," he said.

"How did you know?"

"A lucky guess. When she walked through the front door I pegged her as the reincarnation of a 1960s love child. But despite her eccentricities, I don't get your concern."

Gary rubbed his chin, smearing grease below his lip. "Take a look." He opened the back of the van. "Ms. Chamberlain has been sleeping in the back of her vehicle. On a regular basis. The mattress is well-worn, and she has a stash of personal toiletries in that small cabinet. Call me crazy, but how can a woman like that afford the Silver Beeches? She gave me a platinum card number with no limit. I'm a little spooked though. I can't afford to get ripped off on a job this big."

"Meaning you think the card might be stolen?"

"Well, what's your explanation?"

"I don't have one." Liam's stomach curled with frustration. Had he been taken in by a scam artist?

"How long is she staying?"

"She made a reservation for six weeks."

"Hell, man. You know your rates better than I do. Something doesn't add up."

Liam took one last look inside the van and closed the door. "Go ahead and start ordering parts. I'll cover it all if there's a problem. In the meantime, tell her it's going to be a week or more. I'll offer her a hotel vehicle to drive. That will buy us some time to make sure the credit card is legit." His own motives were muddled, but if he did Zoe a favor, perhaps she would be inclined to drop her guard around him and he could figure out what the hell was going on.

Gary slapped him on the shoulder. "Thanks, Liam. Sorry for interrupting your day, but I thought you'd want to know."

Liam grimaced. "I appreciate the heads-up. I'll keep you posted."

Zoe slept late and enjoyed a wonderfully lazy morning in bed. Breakfast was delivered via room service—a selection of handmade miniature pastries, generous servings of bacon and eggs, and a fancy silver pot full of coffee. By the time she finished, her tummy was uncomfortably full, but she didn't regret a bite of the overindulgence.

Setting the tray outside her door, she made sure the do-not-disturb sign was in place on the doorknob and then climbed back into bed. Because her room was on the top floor, she had the luxury of leaving the drapes open without worrying about anyone looking in on her.

The sunshine boosted her spirits. Pulling the covers up to her chin, she curled into the spot that was still warm and let her mind wander.

She felt safe in this room in a way she hadn't in a long time.

The only shadow over her current happiness was Bessie. The garage owner had called moments before and said the repairs would take a number of days because of the difficulty of getting parts. Which meant Zoe was stranded. The nearest car rental place was at the airport in Asheville. She didn't really want to go back there.

Maybe she could hitch a ride with someone going into town. She liked exploring new places, and Silver Glen, at least from a distance, appeared delightfully appealing.

The severity of her illness had scared her. It was difficult to maintain a healthy lifestyle on the road. Too much fast food and not enough rest and exercise. During the weeks she had booked at the Silver Beeches, she needed to take advantage of the hotel chef's expertise and eat well.

By one in the afternoon, she had reached her limit for *taking it easy.* After showering and changing into black slacks and a silky top with a geometric pattern of taupe and cinnamon, she went in search of the dining room. White linen tablecloths and crystal chandeliers set a standard for elegance, though she saw a wide variety of clothing choices in the diners. Everything from jeans to suits and ties.

Asking the hostess for a table for one did not bother Zoe.

She had lived much of her adult life on her own. Choosing what to order was far more difficult. The menu was amazing. At long last, she settled on chicken marsala with spinach salad and sautéed squash. The meal included hot yeast rolls that were to die for.

As she ate, she studied her companions surreptitiously. Everyone in the room seemed at ease with the upscale setting. No one pretending to be something they were not. But everyone had secrets of one sort or another, no matter their station in life.

She was drinking coffee with her sorbet when Liam strode into the room. He worked the crowd effortlessly, stopping to speak to one table and then another. His confidence and charm drew smiles from patrons who were clearly pleased to receive his attention. Today he wore a navy sport coat over khaki trousers with another crisp white shirt. His tie was a tasteful paisley pattern of blues and greens.

Despite his conservative clothing, his physique was impressive. Broad shoulders, narrow waist and hips, and long legs. If she had to guess, she'd say he was about six-two to her five foot nine.

Zoe smiled at him wryly when he finally made it to where she sat, her pulse skittering in a disconcerting fashion. "You should have been a politician. I can see you kissing babies and shaking hands all over the state."

Without asking, he pulled out a chair and sat down beside her. His quick grin took years off his age. "I hate lying and sucking up to fat cats. So I don't think so. I'm happy right where I am."

"Are you really?"

The grin disappeared, replaced by what she was coming to recognize as his familiar brooding intensity. "What does that mean?"

She shrugged. "Don't you ever have the urge to drive out of town and not look back? Hit the road for places unknown?"

"Is that how you live your life?"

The sharp retort with its hint of disapproval put her back up. "There's a lot to be said for travel. It broadens the mind."

"I've noticed you're good at dodging questions you don't like. Maybe *you* should have been a politician."

She stared at him, nonplussed. Not many people had the sharp wit and the perspicacity to silence her. "Are we having our first fight?"

He shook his head, clearly amused by her question. "I'm in too good a mood today for that. The sun is shining. The stock market is up. The hotel is full. I've got no complaints." He lifted a hand, and the server brought him a cup of black coffee. "I had a phone call from the garage in town," Liam said. "Gary tells me that your vehicle is in the shop. So I've brought you these." He tossed a set of keys on the table.

Eyeing him suspiciously, Zoe ignored the offering. "I've heard of full-service hotels, but this is ridiculous."

Liam leaned back in his chair. "Don't get your hopes up. It isn't a flashy sports car. Just an old Sentra that we keep for the occasional emergency."

"I can't imagine you're this attentive to every guest."

"You'd be surprised. And besides, I have a hidden agenda with you."

Her heartbeat quickened. "How so?"

"My mother accused me of trying to run you off. I need to prove to her that I'm a gentleman. And who knows? You might coax me into playing hooky from work a time or two while you're here."

"You seem like the least likely person I've ever known to be led astray."

"Then you'd be wrong. It's springtime in the mountains. Even a workaholic like me can see the attraction."

When he smiled, ever so gently, Zoe felt something inside her loosen and flower. Despite her tendency to hold people at a distance, something about Liam Kavanagh slipped past her defenses. He wasn't a warm, fuzzy person. In fact, he was rather intimidating. But nevertheless, she felt a strong pull of attraction.

Despite that unsettling truth, she wasn't yet ready to jump headlong into a flirtation that might make her time at the Silver Beeches uncomfortable. She picked up the keys and tucked them in her purse. "Thank you for the vehicle. I'll be careful with it."

He watched her like a cat watches a mouse. "I'm sure you will." After a momentary silence, he continued. "So do you have any specific plans for your stay with us, or are you more the type to be spontaneous?"

"You said that last word as if it put a bad taste in your mouth. Do you have a problem with spontaneity?"

"Not really. Though it isn't an attribute that fits my lifestyle very well."

"Because Liam is all work and no play?"

His eyes narrowed. "You must think me dreadfully dull."

"Not at all. I admire your work ethic."

"Hogwash," he said forcefully, startling her. "You probably don't even own a day planner, do you?" She had the odd notion that he was attracted to her and critical of her at the same time.

She'd been judged and found wanting too many times in her life to let Liam do the same. For the moment, her indignation overrode her appreciation of his masculine appeal. "I believe it's safe to say that our personalities clash, Mr. Kavanagh. Perhaps it might be best if we avoid one another while I'm here. Good day."

With clenched teeth, Liam watched his beautiful guest walk away. The sway of her hips was no less mesmerizing in pants than it had been in a flowing skirt. He had come to the dining room earlier with every intention of getting to know Zoe a little better. Instead, he had lit the fuse of her temper in record time.

Was it the spark of attraction between them that made

things so touchy? Or was Zoe right? Were the two of them oil and water?

Grumbling beneath his breath, he finished his coffee and stood up, ruefully aware that some of the luncheon guests had watched his encounter with interest. Schooling his face to a calm expression, he made his way across the room and exited to the hallway.

Pierre caught up with him en route to the lobby. The longtime employee's face was creased with worry. "There was a man here, Mr. Kavanagh. Asking about Ms. Chamberlain. I got a bad feeling about the guy. Looked like he might be law enforcement or a P.I."

Liam's senses went on high alert. "But he didn't identify himself as such?"

"No, sir. Didn't say much of anything at all except that he was inquiring as to Ms. Chamberlain's whereabouts. At least I think that's what he wanted. He called her Zoe Henshaw, though."

"What did you tell him?"

The concierge's expression was awash with guilt. "I told him we had no guest by that name. He left, but I wondered if I should let Mrs. Kavanagh know."

"I'll handle it," Liam said. "You did the right thing. Our guests expect and deserve their privacy. Keep an eye out for him and let me know if he shows up again."

Liam returned to his office, his gut clenched with worry. Who was Zoe Chamberlain? And why did he feel the need to protect her? Hadn't he learned his lesson long ago? Women were resilient creatures. His need to play Galahad was misplaced at best.

His jaw set, he picked up the phone and dialed the credit card company. After twenty minutes on hold listening to a watered-down version of Frank Sinatra tunes, he was finally connected to a customer service representative who was polite but not at all forthcoming. The woman cited privacy laws, but assured him that the card was not stolen and that the line of credit was unlimited.

Liam hung up and drummed the fingers of one hand on the blotter, no less agitated than he had been before. There was no reason to suppose that Zoe was anything other than an extremely wealthy woman who wanted to spend some time in the mountains.

But somehow, that explanation didn't satisfy him.

Forcing himself to slog through a backlog of work, he made it an hour and a half before he conceded defeat and admitted that the Zoe situation was occupying his attention to the exclusion of all else. Though he would like to think he could let things play out in due time, he knew himself well enough to realize that he wasn't going to be able to let it drop. He had to know more about Zoe. Both for personal and professional reasons. Where was she from? Did she have a job of any kind? Who was the man looking for her? Why did she drive an ancient van, and why was there evidence that at least some of the time, she wasn't sleeping in four-star hotels?

Telling himself that he might be imagining trouble where none existed, he typed the name *Zoe Chamberlain* into Google's search box, hit a key, and waited. To his consternation, the only match from this region of the country was an African-American woman in south Georgia who produced some kind of folk art out of old silverware.

Trying *Zoe Henshaw* produced little else of note. The entries he found contained mostly generic information that could have pertained to any one of a number of people.

Of the Zoe Chamberlain with the golden hair, blue eyes and sunny disposition, there was no mention. Which meant that his oh-so-beautiful hotel guest was probably lying to him. Anger, disappointment, and an amorphous anxiety threatened to choke him.

The Silver Beeches was his turf. Everything that happened beneath this roof was under his domain. Even so, did he have the right to dig into the puzzle that was Zoe? Was he out of line in wanting to find answers?

Six weeks was a long time to wonder.

Four

Zoe loved the little Sentra. It was silver, of course. Although it sported a few dings and bruises, along with 150,000 miles on the odometer, the car had character, much like Bessie. It was also very easy to drive. Its age and appearance erased any concerns she might have had about borrowing someone else's vehicle.

Armed with a map of the town, courtesy of Pierre, she thanked the parking valet who brought the car to the door of the hotel for her. Seating herself behind the steering wheel, she checked the location of all the various knobs and switches and adjusted the mirrors.

If Pierre had thought it odd she was wearing a baseball cap and sunglasses and had her hair tucked back in a ponytail, he gave no sign. The disguise was necessary to calm her nerves.

Driving down the steep, winding highway was an adventure. Like the town itself, the mountain road conjured up images of the Swiss Alps. But the guardrail was sturdy, and the two lanes were plenty wide, so she had no real worries.

The hamlet of Silver Glen was laid out in a well-planned grid tucked between the two steep mountains that constrained its growth. Long and narrow, the peaceful community centered itself along a two-mile stretch of meandering road that wound in a lazy S from one town limit to the other. Cute shops and restaurants vied for space between quaint B and Bs and private homes.

The side streets were equally interesting. Zoe found a dry cleaner's whose sign proclaimed it to be the Silver Press, a movie theater called the Silver Screen, and finally, the place she had circled on her map…Silver Bells, a music shop that sold everything from handmade dulcimers to electronic keyboards.

She spent a happy hour prowling the sheet-music section and debating the merits of a new strap for her guitar. In the end, her only purchase was three sets of replacement strings.

Music softened the rough edges of her life. It was usually easy to strike up a relationship with someone in a new town and offer to play a couple of gigs for free. After that, she was often booked here and there for casual events. She loved being surrounded by the trappings of music. Today she felt a sense of kinship with the little business operated by a man who looked suspiciously like Willie Nelson's twin.

After leaving Silver Bells, she roamed on foot. A shallow river bisected the center of town at right angles to the road. Some long-ago citizens had constructed a covered bridge that was accessible to both cars and foot traffic. Zoe took out her phone and snapped a picture of the postcard scene.

There would be plenty here to keep her busy. Outdoor gear was available in stores everywhere, and the thought of hiking intrigued her. Perhaps she would invest in a good pair of boots.

When the dinner hour approached, she debated returning to the hotel, but she was leery of running into Liam again. She sensed he didn't trust her, and his suspicions stung. Though he was correct to think she was hiding something, it was nothing that would bring harm to his precious hotel. A woman had a right to her secrets, didn't she?

Feeling a bit down in the dumps, she spotted a business that promised to have a decent hamburger on the menu. Making up her mind in an instant, she opened the door and went inside. The Silver Dollar Saloon was dark but smoke-free, a fact that surprised, but pleased her.

Since it was far too early for the locals to really heat up the joint, she was able to grab the booth of her choice. Sitting so that she could look through the front window and study the activity on the street, she perused the limited menu. When the young waitress stopped by, Zoe ordered an Angus burger and sweet-potato fries with a root-beer float.

She took her time soaking in the ambience of the bar. The walls were decorated with black-and-white movie stills, some of them signed. North Carolina was a popular location shoot for producers, and apparently, a number of well-known faces had stopped in at the Silver Dollar to have a cold one at the end of a long day.

The booths that lined both sides of the room looked old. High-backed and made of dark wood, they bore the marks of time. The tables scattered down the center were constructed of the same wood. She almost expected an outlaw or two to come sauntering in.

As she was finishing up her meal, a man appeared from the back, startling her when he stopped at her elbow.

"Welcome to the Silver Dollar," he said. "Haven't seen you in town, so you must be a new visitor."

She looked up, way up, and was surprised to see familiar blue eyes. But the black hair was longer and shaggier. "I'm guessing you might be a Kavanagh," she said.

The man grinned. "Dylan. At your service. I own and operate this place, or perhaps it owns me, if you want to know the truth."

"I'm Zoe Chamberlain."

"So how are you enjoying Silver Glen?"

"I haven't been here long, but your brother is treating me well up at the Lodge."

Dylan raised an eyebrow. "Lucky you. Can't go wrong there." The waitress said something to him, and he started to walk away. "Nice to meet you, Ms. Zoe."

"Wait." The word came out impulsively and with some urgency.

Dylan paused. "You need another root beer?"

"No. I was wondering if you could use a musician one evening. I sing and play guitar. I enjoy doing it, and you wouldn't have to pay me. What do you think?"

His frown didn't say much for her chances. "Aren't you on vacation?"

"Not exactly. I've been ill and I needed a place to rest and recoup. Finding the Silver Beeches Lodge was serendipitous." No need to tell him about Bessie. "I'm going to be here for over a month, and I'm not accustomed to doing nothing all day. It would mean a lot to me. And I'm good, I swear."

Dylan's grin flashed again. Zoe was surprised to realize that, unlike his brother's, Dylan's sexy smile didn't cause her heart to stutter even a little. Apparently she had a thing for irritable, bossy guys in suits. Or at least one in particular.

The bar owner put his hands on his hips and stared at her. It suddenly occurred to Zoe that she wasn't looking her best. Hair tucked back in a ponytail. Well-worn Red Sox cap. He probably thought she was either eccentric or lying about staying up at the Lodge.

Dylan Kavanagh sighed, for the first time sounding much like his brother. "Let me look at the schedule. I have a few bookings coming up. When I know something, I'll call you at the hotel."

She had to be satisfied with that. Even if her hands were already itchy to be playing music. Dylan's bar was exactly the kind of place where she felt most comfortable. "I understand," she said with a smile. "I'll look forward to hearing from you."

* * *

Liam was more than a little surprised when Dylan showed up for a late dinner at the hotel. Maeve and Liam were sitting at a table by the window when his brother appeared. Dylan, wearing a dark sport coat over a pale blue dress shirt open at the throat and neatly pressed jeans, turned female heads as he crossed the room.

Maeve put her hand over her heart. "Dear Lord. It must be a sign of the apocalypse. My second-born son voluntarily dressing for dinner and climbing the mountain without a parental guilt trip."

Dylan bent and kissed his mother's cheek before being seated. "I heard there was prime rib on the menu tonight. You know that's my favorite."

Liam snorted. "You never leave that bar unattended without a good reason. 'Fess up, little brother. Tell us what's important enough to merit such a sacrifice."

"Last time I checked, I had you beat in height by an inch and a half. I haven't been your *little* brother since we both hit puberty, so don't try putting me in my place."

The sibling rivalry was good-natured and familiar. Liam didn't see enough of his brothers, though he loved them all fiercely. Conor and Aidan, and Patrick, Gavin, and James all lived nearby, but the seven brothers led busy lives. For Liam, the hotel was a demanding mistress. Not that it had to be. He employed good people whom he trusted. But perhaps he was too much of a control freak to let them take over.

Maeve beamed at both of them. "Well, whatever the reason, I'm delighted. How did you know when we were eating?"

"I called Pierre and told him I wanted to surprise you."

Liam nodded. "The man can keep a secret. I'll give him that."

The server came to take their order, and the next few minutes were taken up with food choices and wine selection. When the three of them were alone again, Liam sat back in his chair and folded his arms across his chest. "Spill it, Dylan. What brings you up to the rarefied air of the Lodge?"

Dylan's wavy hair was still damp from his shower. He pushed a hank of it off his forehead, pulled his chair closer to the table, and lowered his voice. "I ran into a guest of yours today."

The back of Liam's neck tingled. "Oh?"

"Zoe Chamberlain."

Liam kept his expression neutral, but inside, every Neanderthal impulse he possessed urged him to tell his brother to back off. The lady was taken. That his knee-jerk reflex was ridiculous, he freely admitted. "Where did you see her?"

"She came into the Silver Dollar for an early supper. We chatted for a moment, because the place was mostly deserted."

The salad course arrived, and Liam was forced to hold his tongue for long, frustrating moments while the waiter fussed about with fresh-ground pepper and grated Romano cheese. At last the man departed.

Liam picked up his fork and set it down again. "What did she have to say?" It galled him that his brother had seen as much or more of Zoe today than Liam had. He suspected that she was avoiding him. Without making it obvious, he had looked for her on and off all afternoon. There were a lot of places in the hotel where she could be hiding. The salon, the spa, the workout room, the library. Not to mention the grounds. But he had neither seen her nor heard from her since lunch. Clearly she had made use of the loaner car and decided to go into town.

Dylan chewed and swallowed a bite of his perfectly cooked prime rib, his expression beatific. "I'd forgotten how good this is," he groaned, taking a swallow of his 1972 burgundy. "I love my place, but I'll admit that a guy can get tired of burgers and chicken wings."

Maeve tapped his hand lightly. "I know you pride yourself on being a regular guy, but I happen to know that your bank account could handle a few luxuries. Besides, it wouldn't hurt you to make a standing date with your mother. It's not as if you have any romance in your life at the moment."

"Hey," Dylan said, aggrieved. "That's not fair. I can't help if my girlfriend thought Hollywood was more exciting than a small town in the middle of nowhere."

Liam frowned. Sometimes he thought that Dylan worked too hard at being *one of the guys*. Being a Kavanagh set a man apart in this town. Dylan could fight it all he wanted, but he was a rich man, and people knew it. "Your love life or lack thereof doesn't interest me, no offense. Tell me about your conversation with Zoe."

Dylan kept on eating, apparently intent on clearing his plate in time for dessert. In between bites, he paused to give his brother an assessing glance. "Why so interested? And since when did you get chummy enough with her to use first names?"

Maeve looked from one to the other of her offspring, shaking her head. "I swear you two needle each other every chance you get. I thought you'd grow out of it, but I suppose that was wishful thinking."

Dylan lifted an eyebrow, his smile innocent. "I don't know what you mean, Mom. But you might want to keep an eye on your eldest son. If he starts hitting on sexy hotel guests, we might have problems with jealous husbands."

"Zoe's not married." Liam ground his teeth together, incredulous that his brother's taunts were getting to him. It was an old game they played. But Liam was on a short fuse tonight. "Tell me what you know about her. Please."

Dylan wiped his mouth with his napkin and shrugged. "Not much. But she caught me off guard this afternoon."

"How so?"

"She asked if I would let her play and sing down at the bar."

The table fell silent. Even Maeve seemed perplexed. "Why?"

Dylan shrugged. "Who knows? She claimed it was because she was going to be here for a while and she wasn't used to twiddling her thumbs."

"Did she talk about payment?"

"Offered to play for free."

"What did you tell her?"

"I made an excuse. Said I had to look at the calendar. You know I wouldn't do anything like that without running it by you. Don't want to create a sticky situation. It occurred to me that she might be awful. And that could be damned awkward if she's dropped several grand to stay at the Lodge."

Maeve pursed her lips. "I don't see what it could hurt. She's an unusual woman. Call it my Irish ancestral intuition, but I think she's had a hard life."

Liam and Dylan stared at her in sync. Dylan pointed out the obvious. "She's booked a multiweek stay here at the Lodge. It's not like the woman has lived on the streets and played music so people would toss coins in a tin cup."

Maeve was a levelheaded female, but when she lost her temper, her sons blamed it on the auburn hair that now had touches of gray. "Dylan Matthew Kavanagh. Don't you ever say such a thing again. I thought I'd brought you up better than that. Having money is no guarantee against hardship. The poor girl is all alone on a trip that should be shared by a loved one. We must give her the benefit of the doubt. As our guest, she deserves no less."

Liam winced. "Sorry, Mother. You're right, of course. And as for you, Dylan…" He shot his brother a warning glance. "Let me know what you decide. I want to hear her play."

Dylan nodded, his face sober. "You can tell a lot about a musician through her songs. If Zoe Chamberlain has secrets, they'll be hard to hide when she's onstage."

Liam excused himself shortly afterward. Dylan hadn't been around in a while, so he and Maeve would enjoy catching up. Liam's intent was to go to his office and sift through a pile of paperwork before he headed to bed, but his feet led him in another direction.

The flagstone patio that fanned out from French side doors on the ground floor of the hotel was bathed in moonlight when Liam stepped into the night. Despite the warm day they had enjoyed, here at five thousand feet the temperatures dropped rapidly this time of year after dark.

Almost without realizing it, he turned and began counting windows on the top floor of the hotel until he could locate Zoe's. The drapes were closed. No light emanated from the cracks. Surely she wasn't already in bed. It was not quite ten o'clock.

What had she been up to in the hours since she'd visited Dylan's bar? Lost in thought, Liam wandered the narrow pathways that wove through the gardens like silvery spider webs. His hands linked behind his back, he walked slowly, the pale gravel crunching beneath his shoes. The fragrance of unseen flowers made him think of Zoe.

If he'd been a fanciful man, he would have said that she was very much like a flower—bright and graceful. He wanted to know more about her. In fact, the wanting was more like a gut-level need. It would be hard to sleep knowing that she was at the opposite end of the hallway. He had a suite on the top floor. Maeve went home each night to a modern condo in town.

For the first time that day, he was honest with himself. He wanted to take Zoe Chamberlain to bed. The silent admission sent a rush of arousal coursing through his body. His breathing harshened, and his fists clenched at his sides. Even as he acknowledged his physical need, his brain screamed out a warning. He knew little or nothing about Zoe. It was one thing to be sixteen and infatuated with a woman who turned out to be his father's secret mistress. It was another thing entirely for a mature man to abdicate his responsibilities and throw caution to the wind for the chance to bed a virtual stranger.

What did she look like nude? Her skin would be pale and fine. That much he knew. But what about her breasts? Did the nipples pucker like pink rosebuds when she was excited?

He dropped down onto an ornate concrete bench, his elbows resting on his knees, his head in his hands. Normally, the hotel occupied much of his time and attention. He didn't have hobbies. Occasionally he sought out longtime female friends in other cities for a weekend that satisfied them both. When he did have free time, he loved to be outdoors. But a hotel like the Silver Beeches had to run with precision. Vacationers in this price range expected perfection, or close to it.

Invariably, some crisis erupted once or twice a week. A drunken guest. A falling-out among the staff. A delayed shipment of food. Now that his mother was getting older, Liam tried to spare her the stress and distress of putting out fires. The Kavanagh brothers had lost their father far too soon. Liam wanted his mother to be around for a long, long time.

So he bore most of the burden of being in charge.

Occasionally he resented the yoke of command, but his turbulent feelings were directed at a man who was little more than a ghost in his past. If Reggie Kavanagh had lived, Liam's life would be entirely different. He might be living on the other side of the country, in another part of the world... or possibly even have a family of his own.

Speculation about what might have been was futile. He'd chosen his path. No one had forced him. But sometimes, like tonight for instance, he wished he had the luxury of selfishness at least once in a while.

If he had been a different kind of man, he would run away and join the circus. Sail the seven seas. Learn to speak Swahili. Find out who Liam Kavanagh really was.

But such wild excess was not in his DNA. As a sober, conscientious first child, he was his mother's right-hand man. The rock on which the Kavanagh family anchored its fortunes.

Disgruntled with himself for his maudlin self-pity, he stood abruptly and nearly ran smack into the woman who appeared without warning around a bend in the path. Automatically, his hands came out to steady her. "Zoe. Is that you?"

Five

Zoe gasped, startled and even frightened until she recognized the man who held her lightly. Liam...his face shadowed in the semidarkness. Although the moon was almost full, they were standing amidst large crepe myrtles that cast patterns on the path.

"You scared me to death," she said, feeling her heart thundering away in her chest. "I thought you were a ghost or a rapist or an ax murderer."

"We have so many of those in Silver Glen."

"You're mocking me."

"Maybe. A little." He released her and backed up a step. "Do you mind if I join you?"

She inhaled sharply. Sexual desire. So common and yet so powerful. She shook her head. "Of course not. I only wanted to get some fresh air. I suppose you should lead the way since I don't know where I'm going."

He looked down at her feet. "How are your shoes? Can they handle a bit of rough ground?"

Zoe was wearing the same clothes she'd had on during her excursion into town. The only difference now was that she had omitted the ball cap, and her hair swung free. "I'm good."

"Excellent."

For several minutes they walked side by side, close, but not touching. Eventually, the carefully manicured gardens gave way to forested terrain. Here—the moonlight held at bay by the foliage of large maples—the shadows grew deeper. At one spot where roots humped up in the middle of the trail, Liam took her elbow as they climbed up and over.

He was wearing dress clothes. And presumably his shoes were not meant for such circumstances, but he strode along in the dark easily, his gait comfortable. In this setting, she recognized his athleticism, his grace and power. Alone, she would never have dared go this far in unfamiliar territory. But she knew Liam would not allow her to come to any harm.

Gradually she began hearing the muted roar of water. "Where are we going?" she asked, intrigued and curious.

Even in the dark she saw his grin flash. "To the waterfall."

After that, talking became impractical, because the closer they got to the source, the louder the crash of the torrent.

Finally, Liam took her arm and leaned toward her, his lips brushing her ear. "We won't go any farther. The ledge drops off abruptly."

The silvery moonlight caught the spume and turned it into magic. Shoulder to shoulder, they observed the power of nature. When the wind changed direction, the spray floated toward them, misting their exposed skin and sending a chill down Zoe's bare arms. Liam took off his jacket. Without asking, he tucked it around her shoulders.

The fabric was warm from his body and carried the faint tang of his aftershave. She pulled the lapels closer, wrapped in the majesty of the tumbling water and the simple pleasure of sharing the mystical experience with a man whose company she enjoyed.

At last, when the damp became uncomfortable, Liam took her elbow once again and guided her back into the forest. She tried to return his coat, but he resisted. "Keep it," he said. "Don't want you catching a cold."

When they returned to the more refined landscape of the garden proper, Liam paused, touching her hand briefly. "Would you like to come up to my suite for a drink?"

"And to see your etchings?" she teased.

"Did that line ever work with women, even decades ago? And besides, I would never attempt to seduce a guest with such a corny come-on."

"And if she were willing to be seduced?" The question tumbled out uncensored. Perhaps she'd meant it to be voiced only in her head. But her subconscious was more direct.

They were standing so close, she felt him go rigid. "That's not funny, Zoe."

She leaned into him. "I'm not laughing."

He moved, or maybe she did. Their mouths met clumsily, the shadows making it hard to gauge what was where. Liam's lips were a wonder...firm and warm and confident. Zoe melted, letting him take her weight, straining on her tiptoes to accommodate the insanity.

At last she pulled away. "Coffee would be nice," she said, her breathing ragged. "I'm not much of a drinker."

He stared down at her, the blue of his eyes invisible. But she fancied she could see the turbulence in his azure irises. "Is that a yes?"

"I believe that it is." She tucked her arm in the crook of his elbow. "Will we raise eyebrows sneaking in at this hour?"

"It's hardly late," he said with a chuckle. "And no...we'll take the service elevator." Opening an unmarked side door, he led her down a dimly lit hallway.

She removed his jacket and handed it back to him. "I like the sound of that. Very *crime-drama-ish*."

Liam punched the up button and leaned against the wall

as they waited for the doors to open. "What is this obsession you have with death and dismemberment?"

"The curse of an overactive imagination," she muttered. Now, in the light, she felt a fillip of embarrassment that he was dressed like a man of sophistication, while she was definitely disheveled. She wished she had changed into something sexy and alluring before walking in the garden. Her dark slacks and lightweight blouse were respectable, but hardly the clothing to inspire mad passion.

With a quiet *ding* their clandestine transportation arrived.

The trip was short. But the tension filling the small enclosure multiplied with every second. Unfortunately, this boxy space was not the kind of fancy mirrored affair where a woman could check her reflection.

When they reached Zoe's floor, and what was also apparently his, Liam guided her away from the direction of her room toward his own quarters. Instead of a magnetized card, he had an actual key. Inserting it in the lock, he opened the door and stood back for her to enter.

If she had grown up in less elite surroundings, she would have been awed by the tasteful display of wealth and comfort. Modern, masculine furnishings were softened by warm textiles and the deep pile of moss-green carpeting underfoot. Her toes curled with the urge to kick off her shoes, but she resisted.

Liam loosened his tie and tossed his keys on a narrow table in the foyer. "Have a seat. Make yourself at home. I'll put the coffee on."

"Decaf?"

"If you insist. I'm a night owl, so it doesn't bother me."

She followed him into the kitchen, intrigued.

When he saw her on his heels, he shook his head. "You don't take direction very well, do you?"

"I told you I'm always curious."

While he busied himself with the coffeepot, she examined the amenities. Granite countertops in amber and chocolate tones graced every surface. Over the central island, copper-bottomed pots and pans hung artfully. The stove and refrigerator were a homemaker's dream.

Zoe hopped up on one of the stools that flanked the island and rested her chin on her hands. Liam had rolled up his shirtsleeves, and when he bent over to search the fridge for creamer, his expensive pants molded to a very nice bum.

"This is a fabulous kitchen," she said, seeing herself here, bustling around, making a meal. "Do you like to cook?"

He glanced over his shoulder, grimacing, with his hand on the door of the open fridge. "Actually, I do. But to be honest, it's quicker and easier to eat downstairs. A bad habit, I know."

"I could cook for you one night," she said impulsively. "If you want."

He set the creamer on the island and leaned against the opposite counter, his hands in his pockets. An expensive gold watch gleamed on his left wrist. His hands were big, the fingers long and masculine. Looking at him gave her a funny feeling in the pit of her stomach.

"That would be nice," he said, the inflection neutral.

She flushed, realizing that she was making assumptions. A man like Liam Kavanagh could have any one of a number of women. Standing like that, with a sensual gleam in his eye and the shadow of late-day stubble on his chin, he could have stepped right out of a magazine ad for fast cars or diamonds or gambling in Monte Carlo.

He was beautiful. A beautiful, masculine, physically mouthwatering man.

"Never mind," she said. "You have a five-star chef. I couldn't compete with that."

He lifted one wicked eyebrow. "Oh, I think you could."

Now there was no mistaking his meaning. Liam wanted her.

She swallowed, her voice trapped in her throat. "Is it ready?" she asked, the words squeaky.

"Ready?" He looked blank.

"The coffee."

"Oh...yes."

As he fumbled with mugs and accoutrements, she gathered her composure. "No wonder you never take time off if you *live* here in the hotel. That's a terrible arrangement."

He shrugged, bringing a tray to the island and setting it in front of her. Pulling a stool to the adjoining side, he sat to her right. "The staff is fairly considerate. They try not to disturb me."

"*Try* being the operative word. Don't you ever get the urge to cut loose and be irresponsible?" She stirred a dollop of real cream into her coffee, added a tiny bit of sugar and took a sip. This was no discount-store java. Someone must have ground the beans fresh. It was a luxury she shouldn't get too used to. Her usual M.O. was the drive-through window at McDonald's.

He drained his cup in short order and went back for seconds. "It *is* my hotel," he pointed out as he sat back down. "The buck stops here."

Suddenly, a wave of empathy swamped her. In his own way, Liam was as much of a loner as she was. Both of them surrounded by people much of the time, and yet still lonely. The difference was, Liam had his family nearby. Perhaps they didn't live in each other's pockets, but they were a unit.

Even so, she could see him in her imagination, rattling around in this big, fancy apartment at night with no one to talk to or sleep with. Perhaps he was a workaholic because he had never known anything different.

She had been lost in her thoughts for a long time, because when she finally surfaced, Liam was eyeing her quizzically. "Am I boring you?" he asked, a hint of *something* in his voice that said her checkout had either unnerved or irritated him.

"Sorry."

"What were you thinking about?"

She hadn't expected a direct confrontation, but she should

be learning by now that Liam was nothing if not direct. "Oh, this and that," she said.

Her evasion displeased him. His eyes flashed with irritation. "May I ask you a question, Zoe?"

It wasn't much of a request. More like a command. "I suppose so."

"What do you do for a living?"

Her ankles tightened on the rungs of the stool. "I sing," she said simply. "In nightclubs and bars and coffeehouses. Nursing homes, too, sometimes, but those are freebies."

The intensity of his stare made her want to escape, but she held her ground. She knew what he really wanted to know. His actual question was, how could she afford a six-week stay at the Silver Beeches Lodge if she was an itinerant musician?

But he wasn't rude enough to ask it that way, and she didn't volunteer the information. That was a subject she wasn't prepared to broach. At least not yet.

"I should go," she said, anxiety rising like a dark cloud in her chest. She liked being an anonymous stranger. Perhaps that was why Liam Kavanagh both attracted and threatened her. She sensed that he could break through her inviolable secrets. Walls and barriers and protective shields. She had them all.

"I'm sorry," he said stiffly, his cheeks ruddy with color. "I promised myself I wouldn't pump you for information. It was rude of me."

"Anyone would ask the same question over drinks or on a blind date. Don't beat yourself up because I'm an odd duck."

"Odd, but beautiful."

His honest compliment warmed her. And judging by the look on his face, he had decided he could live with her eccentricities. "I'm harmless, I swear," she whispered.

"That remains to be seen." He smiled to soften the blunt response.

She hopped down from the stool and rubbed her damp palms on her pants. "Thank you for the coffee."

Liam stood as well. "What's your rush? You haven't even seen my etchings yet."

She cocked her head. "I'm assuming you're talking about sex and not real pen-and-ink drawings—right?"

His lips twitched. "A woman who speaks without censoring her words. How interesting."

"Are you calling me a social disaster?"

"On the contrary." He moved closer. "I believe your species might be as rare as the unicorn."

"Don't malign the female sex. Men play games, too."

"How so?"

"Pretending they feel something for a woman when all they want is a quick hookup in exchange for buying her dinner."

He looked at her gravely, his expression guarded. "Unless I'm mistaken, I believe you bought your own dinner. And I haven't been all that interested in quick hookups since I left my grad school days behind."

She bit her lip, feeling outclassed and outplayed. Or perhaps that was a result of her insecurities kicking in. "What do you want from me, Liam?"

His fingers slid beneath her hair as he curled a hand behind her neck. "What do *you* want, Zoe?"

Though the room was plenty warm, gooseflesh broke out on her arms. "Answering a question with a question is classic avoidance behavior."

"But I'm not avoiding you," he said with perfect truth as he pulled her closer still. "You're a guest in my hotel and in my home. I want to please you…to gratify your slightest whim."

It was getting very hard to breathe. The heat from his body melted her synapses, making it impossible to think logically. "I think I read that line from a brochure in my room. Don't oversell the hospitality thing. Zagat won't revoke one of your stars."

He sifted his fingers through her hair. The sensation as his fingertips brushed the skin at her nape was pure pleasure. "You're a bit of a smart-ass, aren't you?"

He didn't appear to mind. If anything her puny resistance had stiffened his resolve. The terrible double entendre, though thank God she didn't say it out loud, sent hysterical laughter bubbling up in her throat. She couldn't quite say when he had managed to pin her body between his big, masculine frame and the refrigerator. Her resistance was crumbling like day-old bread.

"I booked a six-week reservation," she pointed out, panting as he nipped the side of her neck with sharp teeth. "Perhaps we should weigh our options."

Now, his tongue teased the corner of her lips. His breath was warm on her cheek. "How many of our options include my taking you to bed?"

Her knees wobbled. She had started this madness with her flirty question in the garden. *And if she were willing to be seduced?* Liam couldn't be blamed for thinking she was willing and eager to get naked. And she was…sort of….

But in the moonlit dark, with fragrance all around and romance in the air, a woman could understandably rush a few fences. Now she was having second thoughts. And third and fourth.

Caution and common sense came uninvited to the party. If she let this go any farther, Liam would eventually expect to know things about her. Things she wasn't prepared to share. She sighed, arching her neck to give him access to the erogenous zone behind her ear. "Will you think me horribly gauche if I tell you I've changed my mind?" The man had not even kissed her yet, and her stomach was cavorting like a carnival goer on the Tilt-a-Whirl.

She both heard and felt his incredulous groan.

"Not gauche," he grumbled. "Merely frustrating."

Cupping his cheeks in her hands, she petted him like a baby. "Don't be mad, Liam. You should take it as a compliment that you made me lose my senses. I'm rarely so susceptible to blatant romance."

He released her and backed up twelve inches. Bits of his hair stood on end where she had raked his scalp with her fingers. His cheeks were flushed and his pupils dilated. She wasn't even going to acknowledge the way his trousers tented.

Pressing the heels of his hands against his temples, he squeezed his eyes shut. "No sex. I get it."

"No sex, *now,*" she clarified pedantically, not wanting to block the way for future opportunity.

His lashes flew open, his expression fierce as he jammed his hands in his pockets, no doubt to keep from throttling her. "Is kissing on the table? Really long, hot, make-us-both-so-crazy-we'll-never-sleep kisses?"

Licking her lips, she tucked her hands behind her back, her fingertips resting against the cool flat surface of the appliance that was currently holding her upright. What could it hurt? "Of course," she said, as if his question was the most ordinary thing in the world. "Shall I go first?"

Six

Liam knew in that instant that he was either a masochist or the luckiest bastard in the world. And for the moment, he didn't give a damn if Zoe had more secrets than the Sphinx. He cleared his throat. "I'd be delighted for you to go first, Zoe. Be my guest."

She regarded him with big blue eyes, as solemn as a child being offered a treat for good behavior. "I haven't kissed a man in over a year."

"Is that a euphemism for something?"

She shook her head. "No. That other thing you're thinking of is more like a *four*-year dry spell."

"I see." Was she playing him? Could anyone who looked like Zoe and who approached life with such reckless abandon avoid the kind of men who took advantage?

"You don't believe me."

The hurt in her eyes made him feel guilty, particularly since her quiet accusation was well-founded. "I *want* to believe you," he said. "But have you looked in a mirror? Men notice people like you."

"You'd be surprised how well I fly under the radar when I want to. But I understand. You don't know me. And even though you want me, in your gut you think it might be a mistake. You're torn, because you want to kiss me, and that might lead to something else, but you have a family and a hotel to protect. Have I summed it up?"

"I'd like to point out that *you* were the one who changed her mind about sex. Not me."

"Only because I share some of your reservations. Will you take me at my word if I say I have plenty of money to pay my bill? That I'm not a scam artist? Or a criminal of any kind?"

He shifted from one foot to the other, unhappy with the direction the conversation was taking, but reluctant to miss this chance for clarification. "You sleep in the back of your van."

She flushed from her throat to her hairline. Anger? Guilt? He didn't know. A maelstrom of emotions flowed across her expressive features. "Wow. Does everybody in town report to you? Are you some kind of king on the hill?" The sarcasm would have been far more cutting if not for the wobble in her voice.

Weighing his words, he spoke carefully. "My buddy, Gary, is a single dad who struggles to make ends meet. He asked my opinion about whether or not I thought you would stiff him for the repair charges."

Now the color in her cheeks faded, replaced by an aura of despondence. "And what did you tell him?"

Liam shrugged. "I said I'd cover the bill if there was a problem." He was pretty sure he had killed any chance he had of *ever* getting Zoe Chamberlain into bed. At the moment she was looking at him like some wretched creature who had crawled out from under a rock.

She straightened her spine. Moments before, she had been leaning against his fridge, temptation personified. Now her posture defied reproach. "I'll check out in the morning," she said softly, her expression bleak. "Good night, Liam."

Before he could blink, she was out of the kitchen and halfway to his front door. "Wait, damn it," he said, striding after her, his heart pounding. "Don't be ridiculous. Be mad at Gary, but don't be mad at me. I would like to point out, however, that he's a mechanic, not a shrink. It's not like he divulged personal information."

Now her eyes shot blue fire. "Where I sleep *is* personal information. He had no right to tell you that."

Oh, hell. "He didn't exactly *tell* me. He showed me, Zoe. And you certainly don't have to explain if you don't want to. I'm guessing that a handful of the world's richest people do far stranger things. I know personally at least a couple who clip coupons and keep their money in mattresses."

"So now you're calling me crazy, too. Unbelievable."

"You promised to kiss me," he said, desperation making him reckless. Zoe was wearing a sky-blue blouse that deepened the color of her eyes. Her hair was a cloud of sunshine that warmed his dull apartment. Though she was so angry with him she quivered with it, he had never wanted anyone more. "Give me another chance," he pleaded, even knowing in his heart that it was for the best if she walked out. "I didn't set out to violate your privacy, I swear." Reason and sense had left the building.

His passionate entreaty at least slowed her down. "You're not the kind of man to beg," she said. "It doesn't sit well on you."

"Then I won't beg," he muttered. "I'll just do this." Dragging her into his arms, he found her mouth with a shudder that quaked through him like a powerful rift in the earth's core.

If she had fought him, he would have been honor bound to release her. From early adolescence, Maeve Kavanagh had drilled into her boys the proper ways to treat women with respect. She would have Liam's hide for a handbag if she thought he had coerced any female, much less a guest at the Silver Beeches.

Fortunately for Liam, Zoe was not the kind to hold a grudge. She sighed and kissed him back.

Her acquiescence fired his hunger. He gripped her more tightly until she struggled. "Easy, big guy," she said. "I'm not going anywhere. You pled your case persuasively. If this hotel thing doesn't pan out, you ought to think about becoming a lawyer."

"Shut up and kiss me," he cajoled.

Her lips were as soft as the fog that rolled up over the mountain on winter mornings. And she tasted like the best wine in the cellars below. He ran his hands over her back, daring to slide one beneath her shirt. The delineation of her spine was more pronounced than it should have been. Thinking of her so ill bothered him in ways he couldn't explain.

Though her personality was tough, in his arms she seemed fragile, heartbreakingly vulnerable. "I'm sorry," he said again, urging her to believe in his sincerity.

Her waist was narrow, and without a belt, her pants rode low on her hips. Raw need blinded him as he imagined unzipping her clothing, dragging her beneath him and entering her hard and fast in hope of slaking the formidable hunger that gripped him.

Zoe's silence began to worry him. "Say something, damn it."

She tipped back her head and looked him straight in the eye, her expression rueful. "You don't know much about sweet-talking a woman, do you?"

"I've always preferred action to talk. Words can run in circles." Nuzzling her nose with his, he kept his hips pressed to hers, letting her feel what she did to him.

Her arms were wrapped around his neck, gratifyingly

tight. He grasped her chin with one hand, keeping her lips in kissing distance. His other hand fisted in a hank of her hair. Caught thus, she had no choice but to open to him as he gave in to the urge to claim her mouth again.

"Oh, Liam," she sighed. "You do this so very well."

Since he felt like a rank teenager in the grip of angst-laden crush, her words of praise affected him more than they should. "*We* do this well," he corrected. "I'm as surprised as you are." Sliding a hand between their straining bodies, he found a pert nipple and stroked it.

Zoe twined a leg around his thigh. "Don't stop."

"I don't plan to." Scooping her into his arms, he strode toward the sofa, collapsing onto the butter-soft black leather with Zoe in his lap.

She laid her head on his shoulder. "This is the best hotel ever."

"Brat." A wave of tenderness swamped him, for the moment taking the edge off his arousal and allowing his conscience to lobby for maturity and restraint. "You know we probably shouldn't do this, right?"

She sighed. "I know. We've only just been introduced."

"It's not that I don't want to. You are the sexiest, most appealing woman I've ever had the good fortune to meet."

Pulling back to look up at him, she raised her eyebrows. "Ever?"

He grinned, kissing her nose. "Well, I did get introduced to Gwyneth Paltrow once when she was filming a movie here. But movie stars don't count. And besides, she's a little too old for me."

Zoe chuckled, playing with a button on his shirt. "You're telling me you wouldn't have carnal relations with Gwyneth Paltrow if you had the chance?"

"Chris Martin might not like it."

"He's a musician. You're a wannabe football player. I think you could take him."

Fighting his baser instincts, he stood up, setting her on

her feet and moving himself out of temptation's reach. "If you stay here any longer, we both know what's going to happen. As much as it pains me to point it out, I think the timing is wrong. You said so yourself."

Folding her arms across her chest, she regarded him with stormy eyes. "If you think I do this with everyone I fancy, you'd be wrong. I was serious about the four-year thing."

"Then why me?" It was a legitimate question, not false modesty.

Her shoulders lifted and fell. "I don't really know. Your brother looks a lot like you, but I didn't get the urge to drag him into bed."

Liam was torn between relief and irritation. "Dylan says you want to play at his bar."

"Yes."

"And again, why?"

"I enjoy music. Is that so hard to understand?"

He knew she was hiding things about herself. And wasn't trying very hard to pretend otherwise. A sense of foreboding overtook him. Though he claimed to be pragmatic, he did, after all, have several hundred years of Irish blood flowing in his veins. There was no denying the occasional frisson of gut feeling that guided his actions.

"A man was here today," he said quietly. "Looking for *you*. Or rather, *Zoe Henshaw*. Since *Zoe* is a fairly uncommon name, Pierre and I assumed he meant you."

She dropped abruptly onto the sofa…as if her legs had simply folded beneath her. Every ounce of color leached from her face. "Who?"

"I don't know. Pierre dealt with him. The man didn't identify himself."

"What did Pierre tell him?" She looked as if the answer might be a knife to her chest.

"That we had no guest by that name. Then the guy left. We take privacy very seriously here, Zoe. You're safe. For however long you choose to stay at Silver Beeches." He would have written the vow in blood if it could have removed the look of panic and despair on her face. "Talk to me," he said softly. "I won't betray your trust."

Zoe read the sincerity in his face, the masculine urge to help. But she dared not let down her guard. "Thank you," she said quietly, wondering if she was capable of standing up. "But I'm fine."

Her answer visibly displeased him. "Do you know who it was?"

"No." God, it horrified her to realize how easy it was to lie. But keeping her own counsel had been her only protection in the last year and a half. "Thank you for telling me."

She forced herself to rise and move toward the door. It was foolish to think she could afford a relationship with Liam Kavanagh, no matter how tempting he was. The only person she could trust, in the end, was herself. "I enjoyed the waterfall," she said quietly, her hand on the doorknob.

Liam remained where he was. Clearly, this time he had no plans to stop her. The inscrutable expression on his face probably meant he was relieved to have dodged a bullet. Zoe came with baggage. Most men wanted easy sex with no consequences.

His nod was jerky. "My pleasure."

"Good night." Out in the hall, she leaned her head against the wall, her heart beating wildly. The urge to flee was strong. But she had no vehicle. Taking the little Sentra was not really an option. Even if she left behind the money to pay for it, she would not have the title. Through the years she had done a couple of things she was not proud of, but she drew the line at stealing a man's car. Even if it *was* a clunker.

Being alone in the world had its drawbacks. She envied Liam his close-knit family. She'd never had that kind of support growing up, and as long as she forced herself to keep running, she would never have a shot at the kind of roots and permanence she saw in Liam.

Wiping her damp eyes with the back of her hand, she sought out her peaceful room. With the door locked behind her, she took a deep breath. Tomorrow she would make a plan.

Liam paced his roomy apartment for an hour after Zoe left. Not only was he experiencing the aftereffects of their aborted intimacy, he was also worried. Deeply worried. Zoe was in trouble of some kind. Big trouble.

It wasn't Liam's problem. He kept telling himself that, even as his brain wrestled with the question of how to get her to trust him. On the surface, her personality was open and sunny. But dig a little deeper and you found a woman who resembled a house of mirrors. Just when he thought he had a clear idea of who she was, he ran into a dead end.

Glancing at the clock, he decided it would be okay to call his night-owl brother.

Dylan answered on the second ring. His voice was louder than usual, obviously struggling to be heard above the noise in the bar. "What's up? Didn't I just have dinner with you a few hours ago?"

"I've changed my mind."

"About what?"

"I wasn't sure before, but now I want you to invite Zoe Chamberlain to sing at the Silver Dollar. The sooner the better."

"What's the emergency?"

Liam laughed roughly, digging the heel of his free hand into his eyes one at a time. "I wish I knew. Our beautiful guest is in some kind of trouble. I don't know more than that. But I want to hear her sing. Is that a problem?"

"Of course not. I'll call in the morning and tell her we'll put together a set for tomorrow night. Will that do?"

"Yeah. Thanks, Dylan."

His brother's voice was wry. "You picked up the pieces when I was a mess. The least I can do is lend a hand with your new girlfriend."

"She's not my girlfriend," Liam said automatically. He wasn't sure how to categorize what he felt for Zoe, but he was pretty damned sure their situation was nothing as simple as that.

"Well, whatever she is, I hope she can sing. My regulars have been known to harass the few duds I've had."

"If she says she can sing, I believe her. I plan to bring her down to the saloon and stay with her. What time are you going to tell her to be there?"

"We'll need a few minutes to talk about songs. Do you want to grab a burger while you're here, or is that too plebeian for your refined palate?"

"You're such an ass. And yes. A burger sounds great."

"Seven o'clock, then. After we eat, I'll take her in the back for a few minutes and work on the set list."

Liam cleared his throat. "I think dinner will be just Zoe and me. No offense."

A second of silence stretched to two and then three. Dylan's response, when it finally came, was hushed. "Ho-lee shee…it. Has my mighty brother fallen for a tourist?"

"Mind your own damn business. And just for the record, I'll be joining you *in the back*."

"Message received. But you don't really think I'd poach on your territory, do you bro?"

"Do you remember Pamela Fletcher back in middle school?"

Dylan chuckled. "Point taken. But I've matured since then."

"Says who?"

"Ask anybody. I'm an upstanding businessman."

"An upstanding businessman with an eye for the ladies."

"I've reformed, I swear."

"In all seriousness, Dylan, help me keep an eye on Zoe. Some guy was here at the hotel today asking about her. Pierre told him flat out that no such person had checked in."

"Go, Pierre. He takes his job seriously."

"We all do. And apparently this unwanted visitor gave off enough of a bad vibe for Pierre to be suspicious."

"Does Zoe know about the visitor?'

"Yes."

"Be careful, Liam. You can't always save the world."

Liam winced, feeling something a lot like hurt. "Am I really such an insufferable prig?"

Dylan's voice lowered to a more normal level. Presumably he had stepped into his office, because the background noise disappeared. "That's not what I said, or what I meant. You've sacrificed for all of us, and we're damned grateful. But sometimes you take on too much responsibility. You need to lighten up and live a little. If this Zoe gal is too complicated, find somebody else. But get laid and quit worrying."

"I can't believe I'm taking relationship advice from my baby brother."

"You could do worse. I've survived the pitfalls. I'm a cautionary tale."

"I don't think anything is going to happen with Zoe."

"But you want it to."

"Maybe." That was as honest as Liam was willing to be.

"I'll help you watch out for your little chick, I promise. But Liam…"

"Yeah?"

"Be careful. Just because she looks like an angel doesn't mean she is one."

Dylan had been deceived once upon a time by a woman with a pretty face and a cold heart. The experience hit him hard, and at no point since had he allowed any woman to get close to him. He was understandably cynical when it came to the opposite sex.

"I don't want to believe Zoe is a threat. I'm more concerned about a potential threat to her."

"Then we'll both be on the lookout. I'll see you tomorrow night."

"Thanks. I owe you one."

Seven

Zoe's stomach fluttered with nerves. Which was disconcerting, because she was rarely unsettled before a show. It usually took her father's goons a few weeks to find her latest bolt-hole. The fact that someone had come looking for her so quickly was alarming. But Pierre had sent the stranger away. Convincingly. So she was safe…for now. Perhaps her unusual restlessness could also be attributed to the fact that a polite bellman had delivered a note to her room an hour ago.…

> *Dear Zoe—*
> *I'd like to accompany you to the Silver Dollar Saloon*
> *tonight, if I may. Meet you in the lobby at 6:30? Call*
> *the front desk and leave me a message. Liam.*

She had tucked the note in a drawer of the bedside table. Now she took it out and studied it again. Liam's bold scrawl was neat, though masculine. She could almost see him writing the words, in a hurry to get on to the next thing, but still concerned with making sure she had a ride into town tonight.

She had danced around her suite when Dylan called earlier. Given the bar owner's reaction yesterday, it seemed safe to assume she'd never hear from him. But not only had he called, he wanted her to perform tonight. With him. For the crowd at the Silver Dollar.

The whole thing had her jazzed and excited until Liam's note arrived. Was it possible to experience stage fright in front of only one person? She was confident about her talent, but what if she had an off night? What if she hit a couple of sour notes? Or sang in the wrong key? The prospect of appearing amateurish with Liam watching made her stomach curl with dread.

Unfortunately, she was unable to think of a polite way to tell him she would prefer he stayed home. Thus at 6:25, she made her way downstairs. As she stepped off the elevator, she spotted Liam immediately. He stood on the far side of the lobby conversing with Pierre.

Though he wasn't wearing jeans, he had clearly dressed for an occasion less upscale than dinner at Silver Beeches. A pale blue button-up shirt with the sleeves rolled to his elbows exposed his tanned forearms and strained across his broad shoulders. Light khaki pants and leather deck shoes completed his ensemble. Even dressed casually as he was, he still looked wealthy and powerful. His impact was in the set of his jaw and the aura of command he wore so comfortably.

When Liam saw her approach, he said something to Pierre and crossed the marble floor. "Zoe. You look amazing."

Liam struggled to keep his tongue from dragging the floor. It had been almost a full day since he had seen her, and his imagination had not exaggerated her appeal. Silky sunlit hair framed a face that was both girl-next-door and sex goddess. He wasn't sure how the combination worked, but it made him hotter than hell.

He didn't know what he had expected in terms of her performance attire. But she had surprised him. Dark-wash jeans fit her long, toned legs as if they had been sewn onto her. A narrow brown leather belt cinched her small waist. The silver and turquoise buckle was delicate and intricate.

Her blouse was the ultimate feminine weapon…a collarless, sleeveless red silk affair that clung to her breasts and tucked neatly into her jeans. He didn't count how many buttons had been left undone, but the rounded slopes of her cleavage were tastefully displayed.

The simple gold chain that encircled her neck nestled in the valley between her breasts. On narrow, high-arched feet she wore red stilettos that brought her almost up to his height.

He knew that he had never seen a sexier, more sensual woman.

His voice was embarrassingly gruff when he spoke a second time. "Are you ready to go?"

She nodded, her smile small, but genuine. "I am."

He took her elbow as they stepped outside. His classic silver Jag convertible, circa 1962, waited for them, engine running. After helping Zoe into the passenger seat, he put her guitar case in the back, ran around the car, and slid behind the wheel. "I decided to keep the top up since you're performing tonight. But one afternoon soon I'll take you for a drive in the mountains."

"Sounds lovely."

It was difficult to believe they had almost made love last night. Though Zoe had pulled away, he knew she wanted him. Perhaps a slow wooing was in order. For a skittish woman with defensive walls, a man needed tact and patience. Liam had both. And he was willing to do almost anything to lure Zoe into his bed. Wise or not, he had no choice. The wanting and the waiting were eating him alive.

The atmosphere today was definitely strained. He decided it was better to say nothing at all as they descended the mountain. Zoe was probably getting in the groove for her performance. And besides, he couldn't verbalize what he was really thinking. She would no doubt run away if she had a clue what he wanted from her.

He nearly clipped a guardrail when she crossed her legs and one of her call-girl shoes fell to the floor of the car. Her toenails were painted to match the vibrant color of her outfit. Though he had never once entertained a foot fetish, he had a sudden vision of lying naked in bed with Zoe, sucking each of those small perfect toes one at a time.

In his peripheral vision he saw her grimace as she replaced her shoe. "It's very kind of your brother to let me perform tonight. He's taking me at my word that I can sing."

"Were you exaggerating when you described your performance experience?"

"No."

He patted her knee, removing his hand quickly when the contact threatened to singe his fingertips. "Then you have nothing to worry about. Dylan knows how to loosen up a crowd, and even if you were the worst singer on the planet, I guarantee you that the clientele at the Silver Dollar will cut you some slack when they get a look at those jeans."

She turned toward him, her bottom lip caught between her teeth. "Are they too tight? I forgot how much I've eaten since I've been here. I guess I've already put on a pound or two."

"The jeans are perfect." End of story. A few moments later, he swung into the back parking lot of the saloon and rolled to a stop beside his brother's vehicle in the space that was always saved for family. "You want to go in, or do you need a minute?"

Clasping her hands in her lap, Zoe inhaled sharply. "I feel like I might throw up. But I think that's because I don't usually know anyone in the audience."

He ran the back of his hand down her cheek, feeling his gut tighten from that simple contact. "Are you saying that I make you nervous, Zoe?" The prospect delighted him, because it meant she was as attuned to him as he was to her.

"No comment." Her expression was rueful.

"You're the one who asked to sing here," he pointed out.

"And now I want to get it over with."

"Then let's find my brother."

The Silver Dollar was already packed. The hostess greeted them warmly and gave Liam a smack on the lips. "Where you been keeping yourself, gorgeous? I've missed you."

Delilah was twenty years his senior and thirty pounds overweight. But her exuberant personality drew men like bees to honey. He squeezed her arm. "Behave, Dee. Meet my friend, Zoe. She's going to sing with Dylan tonight."

Delilah stepped back and examined Zoe from head to toe. To Zoe's credit, she withstood the other woman's scrutiny without flinching. Delilah shook her head. "Where'd you get this exotic creature, Liam?" Then she smiled at Zoe. "You're a knockout, honey. Call me Dee."

Dylan showed up at that moment and took over the task of ushering them to a table. He had reserved one for them in the back. The cramped space was the closest the Silver Dollar came to privacy. A scraggly artificial tree served as a partial barrier between Liam and Zoe and the other diners.

Despite Liam's warning stare, Dylan seated himself at Zoe's elbow. He handed her a slip of paper. "Do you know any of these?"

She examined the list with a dawning smile. "Only all of them."

Dylan beamed. "Have your dinner, then, and afterward we'll do a quick run-through and take the stage around 8:30. Sound okay to you?"

Zoe nodded, her blue eyes sparkling. "Perfect."

Thankfully, Dylan took himself away and Liam was left

to entertain Zoe. "I can recommend the hot wings and the jalapeño poppers," he said, wondering how many hours it would be before he could take another shot at convincing her to be alone with him. And naked.

Zoe studied the menu with suspect concentration. She was jumpy as a cat with a mangled tail. Whether it was from being with him or the result of stage fright, he couldn't tell.

After they ordered, they watched the crowd. Zoe pointed to a large man wearing nothing but red suspenders and threadbare painter's pants. "Who is that guy?"

Liam took a swallow of his imported ale and grinned. "Big Tom. For most of the year he runs a sawmill outside of town. But from Thanksgiving to Christmas, he works at a mall in Asheville every year as Santa Claus."

"I can see why."

Big Tom's gut was hard to miss. Daring to change the subject to a more personal note, Liam stroked the back of her hand lightly where it lay on the table. "I'm sorry we argued yesterday."

Zoe's makeup was more dramatic tonight, which made sense, because she planned to be onstage. But her thickly mascaraed lashes, lowered to half-mast, shielded her eyes. She withdrew her hand. "It's okay."

"It's *not* okay. You're entitled to your secrets. But if I'm being completely honest, I hope that you'll eventually figure out that you can trust me."

"Trust is a two-way street."

"Indeed. But you make it difficult. *Chamberlain* isn't your real name, is it?"

She shot him a mutinous glance. "Yes it is. But it's my middle name. I use it for everything. That's not a crime the last time I checked."

"Zoe, I'm not attacking you. I want to help. Who is the man who's looking for you?"

"I don't know." Shoulders hunched, her body language screamed at him to back off.

She was lying. He knew it in his gut. But he wasn't willing to make a scene in Dylan's bar. Especially when Zoe was about to be in the spotlight…literally.

It went against his every instinct, but he swallowed his frustration and conceded that now was not the time for a confrontation. Their food arrived, and the moment was lost.

When Dylan came to get Zoe for their mini run-through, Liam gave his brother a pointed stare. "Your office is small. I'll stay here and check a few emails."

Dylan nodded, for once, his expression not teasing at all. "We won't be gone long. Tell the server if you want anything else."

Scanning the room for anyone who might resemble the man Pierre saw, Liam sat back in his chair and relaxed a bit. No one could harm Zoe in the middle of a crowd like this. He ate a few French fries as he scrolled through messages on his phone.

When someone sat down beside him, he looked up with a smile. Until he saw that it was Gary. And Gary looked far too serious.

The mechanic spoke in a low voice. "Is she here?"

Liam nodded. "In the back with Dylan. The two of them are performing together tonight. What's up?"

"I sure the hell don't know."

"Tell me, man. She'll be back soon."

Gary pulled his chair closer and lowered his voice. "She called this morning and asked if I would paint her entire vehicle brown. When I finished the other repairs."

"So?"

"Her current paint job is almost brand-new. Nary a ding or a scratch. The only reason I can come up with for covering over her daisies and all the rest is that she doesn't want to be spotted."

Liam's stomach churned. He didn't want to believe that his friend had a valid point. "Isn't that jumping to conclusions?"

Gary shook his head. "There's more. I decided to prep the vehicle since I'm waiting on parts. I found a small area of rust around one door hinge, so I removed the door. The inside panel seemed loose. I was going to fix it, when I found…"

He paused as the waitress refreshed their drinks.

Liam's neck was tight. "What, damn it? What did you find?"

"Money." Gary grimaced. "Lots of money. Cash. Bills."

"How much?" God in heaven.

"I don't know. I didn't touch it. Didn't want my fingerprints to show up anywhere. But I'd say at least forty or fifty thousand given the denominations and the size of the stacks." He paused, his expression torn. "Do you think I should call the police?"

Liam ran a hand over his face, his brain assessing and discarding a dozen possible explanations. "No. We have no proof that it's not hers." Hope curdled in his stomach and died. He'd tried so hard to tell himself that Zoe was trustworthy, and now this.

"Who carries that much cash hidden in a vehicle?"

"I don't know," Liam said grimly. "But I plan to find out."

Zoe strummed a chord as Dylan tuned his guitar. His instrument was beautiful. Highly polished wood inlaid with silver in random designs. "Did you have that made?" she asked.

He nodded, still fooling with one of his strings. "Yeah."

"Does the silver design have some special significance?"

"It reminds me that I'm a Kavanagh for good or for ill. Once upon a time our ancestors operated a silver mine in these mountains, hence the name of the town. We have a few large remnants, good-size nuggets, but the mine was lost years ago. Our father disappeared while looking for it when Liam was in high school. Not only did Dad never find the mine, he never returned."

"That's dreadful." Zoe could hardly imagine a tragedy of that magnitude, though her own family life hadn't been a picnic.

"A dark time in the Kavanagh clan, for sure. As the eldest, Liam bore the brunt of helping Mom cope. He was always mature for his age, but he had to grow up overnight."

"How did she manage when he was away at university?"

"We hired an assistant manager. Mom was in charge, but there was someone to help with the big decisions. And Liam would come home from school if he was needed."

"So he never got to go backpacking through Europe or take a graduation trip or anything like that?"

"No. And by the time our collective grief eased and things were finally on an even keel, both personally and professionally, Mom had come to depend on Liam. In case you hadn't noticed, my brother is the kind of man people turn to for support. In one way or another, he's been the cornerstone of our family for twenty years now."

"How old were you when it happened?"

"Fourteen. I'm the next in line. But there's a lot of difference between fourteen and sixteen. I was going through a rebellious phase, and Dad's death only made things worse."

Zoe fell silent, digesting the implications of what Dylan had shared. No wonder Liam had such a serious side. He hadn't had the luxury of being a goofy adolescent. Her admiration for him grew, along with the conviction that she was not the woman to get involved with him. If he knew the extent of her problems, she would become one more millstone of responsibility hanging around his neck.

Dylan finished tuning. "You feel okay with what we've sketched out?" he asked with a smile.

"Yes. I hope I don't disappoint you." It still amazed her that his sexy masculinity didn't affect her libido the way Liam's did. Some woman would be lucky enough to fall for Dylan Kavanagh one day in the future. But apparently Zoe had already cast her lot with the straight-laced older brother.

Dylan straightened his guitar strap around his neck, resting his arm on the instrument. "Now that I've heard your voice, I'm wondering how I can convince you to be a regular."

"That's very kind of you. But I won't be hanging around more than a few weeks."

"Why not?"

His simple question caught her off guard. Why not, indeed? Her gypsy lifestyle was her own choice. No one was making her crisscross the country and live out of a single suitcase. Only her cowardice and fear pushed her onward. "I suppose I've never liked being tied down."

Her answer didn't satisfy him. His unspoken empathy made her squirm. "Nobody can run forever," he said. "Trust me. I know."

"Who says I'm running?"

"Aren't you?" In his steady gaze she saw a kindred spirit.

Her throat tightened unexpectedly, leaving her to blink back emotion. "I'm not sure I would know how to put down roots after all this time. I don't make friends very easily."

"And yet you're around people all the time when you're playing and singing."

"That's different. I can blend into the background."

"I think you're kidding yourself." His measured look was not insulting, but her cheeks heated. She glanced at her watch. "Is it time?"

He nodded. "You feelin' butterflies?"

"A million of them," she confessed.

Dylan stood and patted her shoulder. "I know my regulars. They're going to love you. Come on, Ms. Zoe Chamberlain. Let's go make some music."

She stood as well and wiped her damp palms on the legs of her jeans. "I'm ready. Let's do this."

Eight

The stage at the Silver Dollar was tiny, but Liam's brother had invested in a top-notch sound system and professional lighting. The house lights had already been lowered, so when Zoe stepped out onto the stage, a few steps ahead of Dylan, the audience made an audible sound of appreciation.

Even though Liam knew what she looked like tonight, he caught his breath along with the rest. She was radiant. Her smile, intimate and happy, encompassed the crowd, telling them that they were part of her inner circle and that she would be singing just for them.

Two stools sat side by side on the stage. Though Dylan sat down beside Zoe, Liam scarcely gave his brother a glance. It was safe to say that all the men in the room reacted similarly.

Zoe perched comfortably, her hair swinging softly around flushed cheeks. Her eyes sparkled, and her slender body practically vibrated with excitement. She wrapped her ankles around the rungs of the stool. In that one movement, Liam flashed back to sitting with her in his kitchen.

Dylan leaned toward his mike. "Welcome, regulars and first-time visitors to the Silver Dollar Saloon. Glad you're all here. We have a treat in store tonight. My friend, Zoe, is going to sing and play with me. She's just passing through Silver Glen, but I was able to persuade her to entertain us this evening. Please give it up for Zoe's first performance at the Silver Dollar."

After the raucous whoops and hollers quieted, Dylan began to pick out a melody, and Zoe joined in. In no more than a few seconds, the room fell silent, all rustling and coughing and other noises obliterated.

Liam had heard his brother sing and play a million times. Dylan was talented, and touched his guitar like he would a woman, with tenderness and reverence. He had the Irish gift of storytelling in song.

But with Zoe on stage as well, Dylan became the background to her luminance. They started out with the poignant lyrics to an old sixties tune about difficult goodbyes. With a jolt of distress, Liam saw Zoe standing at his bedroom door, her bags packed, not wanting to wake him up to say goodbye. The image was so vivid, for a moment he couldn't breathe.

The first time he met her, she had struck him as the reincarnation of a sixties love child, guitar in hand. Now, singing words that had resonated for decades, he felt as if all the grief of parting washed over him, though she hadn't even thought about leaving yet.

And somehow, Liam's father swam into the mix. Reggie Kavanagh had left, never to return. If Liam hadn't been sitting so far from the door, he might have cut and run. He wanted to howl with the knowledge that he was halfway in love with Zoe already and already bracing for the pain of a broken heart.

Fortunately for him, after one or two more ballads about being sad and lonely, Dylan launched into a crowd pleaser, and soon everyone was clapping hands and singing along. Several modern country songs followed.

Liam wasn't sure how long Dylan and Zoe played. No one left the bar. Waitresses worked the crowd, pausing now and again to watch and listen. The upward curve of Dylan's lips told Liam his brother was in his element. But it was the sheer joy on Zoe's face that kept the crowd in their seats. She sang from the heart, as if every emotion she had ever experienced could be communicated in song.

At last, Dylan announced the last number. "Zoe's going to sing and play for us an original composition. We're pleased you were here tonight, and we hope you'll return. Good night and God bless."

The spotlight trained on Dylan's stool went out. He was still there to play, but all attention focused on Zoe. At this moment, she no longer seemed aware of the audience. With her head bent over her instrument, she strummed the opening bars of a haunting tune. When she opened her mouth to sing, she captured each listener in the palm of her hand.

With a voice that was husky and pure, she sang of love and loss and the universal pain of a broken heart....

"I never meant to hurt you...loving is a fearful game...
Few can win and most go home
Facing winters of the same...

"I thought we might be different...or at least we'd have a chance...
But life is not a promise
And I scarcely know the dance.

"Don't grieve long for might-have-beens...remember me with wonder
Like new roses crushed by rain
Our future's torn asunder...

"Goodbye, my love, so perfect...please forgive my gift of pain...

If I could stay, I would have
Always will my love remain...."

The final note of the final verse lingered on a hushed silence. Liam heard sniffles and saw women wiping their eyes.

Though he knew, intellectually, that Zoe was blinded by the spotlight shining in her eyes, it seemed to him as if she looked straight at him, sending him a message. *Don't care about me. Don't fall for me.*

What she didn't know was that it was too late. He wanted her with a desperate urgency that left no room to contemplate any ending other than a happy one. If Zoe was in trouble, he would help her. Even if she turned out to be a thief. He had to believe there were reasons for whatever she had done to get that money. He would stand by her. And when the danger had passed, he would bind her to him and shred the music to that dreadful song.

He might be making a mistake. In fact, he was *probably* making a mistake. But he was ready to suffer the consequences. He was prepared to do almost anything as long as it meant he could have Zoe.

While his emotions swirled from pride in her talent to frustration at her secrecy, the crowd rose as one to its feet, clapping and whistling and demanding an encore. At Dylan's signal, the house lights came back up and Dylan and Zoe launched into a rowdy, energetic rendition of an old Billy Ray Cyrus tune.

Afterward, Dylan gave Zoe a hug and insisted she take a bow. Her face was flushed and damp, and for the first time, she looked tired. Suddenly, Liam remembered that she had been ill. Working his way to the front of the stage, he handed her a bottle of water.

"Drink something," he said quietly. "You may have overdone it tonight."

When she had emptied the bottle, he held up his arms and lifted her down from the stage onto the plank flooring.

"Thank you," she said, not meeting his eyes.

When Zoe would have moved away, he stopped her by the mere expedient of keeping his arms looped around her waist. "Take a breath, sunshine. You were a big hit."

She rested her head on his shoulder. "Great audience."

He heard fatigue in her voice alongside the satisfaction of a job well done. "You ready to go home?" The words slipped out before he had a chance to censor them. The Silver Beeches was *his* home, not Zoe's.

She didn't call him out on his faux pas. "More than ready. But it was a great night."

Dylan walked them out to the car. "You were a hit, Zoe. I hope you'll plan to do this again. But I only accept a freebie once. I'd have to pay you from now on."

"You couldn't afford me," she said, laughing. Liam couldn't see the mischief in her eyes, because it was dark now. The only illumination came from the multicolored lights strung along the roofline of the Silver Dollar.

Liam helped Zoe into the car and turned to his brother, lowering his voice. "Call me in the morning. I need your advice about something."

Dylan snickered. "I say go for it."

Liam slugged his arm and slid into the driver's seat. "Good night, Dylan."

Zoe leaned across his lap to add her goodbyes. Her breasts brushed his chest, and her hair tickled his chin. "Thanks for letting me sing."

Dylan leaned on the window. "My pleasure. You kids get on home now. It's late."

"You're so full of it." Liam hit the up button on the window, causing his smart-ass brother to jump back with a curse.

Zoe giggled, straightening and returning to her own seat as Liam exited the parking lot with a flurry of gravel. "That was mean. But funny."

"My brother is a merciless tease. Be glad he likes you."

"He likes everybody, it seems. The bar was packed tonight. And I think he knew everyone there."

"That's Dylan."

Conversation lagged abruptly. Liam drove with an occasional surreptitious glance at the slightly rumpled and definitely weary angel occupying the passenger seat of his car. Near the top of the mountain there was a pull-off where the teenagers liked to park and make out. The idea had definite appeal. But what he wanted to do with and to Zoe required far more privacy.

He still hadn't decided what to do about Gary's latest revelation. There could be a hundred reasons why Zoe was hiding large amounts of cash in the panel door of her van. Unfortunately, a lot of them were worrisome.

Back at the hotel, Liam handed his keys to the valet and helped Zoe out of the car. It occurred to him that they could take a walk as they had the night before. But she had expended a lot of energy onstage, and she probably intended to have an early night.

He wanted to talk to her, to convince her they belonged together, even if for only this moment in time. And if she agreed to make love to him, he had to seek answers that would make him feel better about having her in his hotel and in his bed. Every time he had tried before, she shut him out. Bracing himself for the disappointment of a quick goodnight as a prelude to her disappearance, he walked beside her into the lobby, carrying her guitar case.

Making an excuse to go to his office would save him the awkwardness of riding up on the elevator with her, but he couldn't bring himself to walk away. On the top floor, the door opened, and they both stepped into the quiet hallway.

Zoe held out her hand for the instrument. "Thanks for going with me tonight."

To hell with this. He set the case on the floor and reached for her. "You mesmerized me with your singing. One kiss. That's all I need."

It was a lie. He knew it and she knew it. What he wanted would take all night. Given their semi-public location, he held her loosely, not wanting to embarrass her if another guest decided to walk by. He slid both hands beneath her hair, inhaling her scent as he bent his head and found her mouth. "You were amazing," he muttered, moving his lips over hers with light, teasing motions.

Zoe went up on tiptoe, her arms twined around his neck as she kissed him back. "That's sweet of you to say."

"I'm not a sweet man." He caught her tongue between his teeth and nipped it to prove his point. Zoe's soft moan hit him hard, stealing the breath from his lungs and weakening his knees, even as another part of him went hard as stone. He shook with the need to take her up against the wall.

"Come to my room," she whispered.

He froze, sensing some kind of test, or perhaps a trap. "I can't," he said hoarsely. "Not now. Not tonight. I'm past talking." He cupped her butt in those body-hugging jeans and squeezed it. "If I get you alone, there's only one thing that's going to happen. Fair warning."

She tilted her head to look up at him, her guileless blue eyes impossible to read. "I don't have a problem with that, Mr. Kavanagh."

The time for rational thought was long past. He had been imagining this moment since the first instant she stepped through the door of his hotel. What did it matter if her presence was only temporary? Why did he care if she was frustrating and secretive and slept in her van and had loads of hidden cash and people looking for her?

He wanted her. He needed her. And by God, he was going to have her.

Taking her by the hand, he grabbed the guitar case and strode down the hall, dragging Zoe in his wake. It took her several seconds to rummage in a small bag for her key. He didn't bother to tell her he had a master key that gained him access to every room in the hotel. This way was better.

Inside her room, he set her instrument in front of the closet and leaned against the door, doing his best not to pounce on her. Her red blouse was rumpled, her hair mussed. "I suppose you want a shower," he said, trying to be the gentleman his mother had taught him to be.

Zoe grimaced. "I need one. But there's room for two."

His vision hazed. Hands trembling, he stared at her. "You have to be sure, Zoe. No backing out at the last minute. It's okay to say no, but I want to hear it now."

She frowned, the movement creating two small lines in her forehead. "I believe I invited you to my room. That's a pretty clear signal in my book."

"We're practically strangers."

"I don't care."

"You're not sure you can trust me."

"And vice versa. But this is about sex."

"And if either of us wants more?"

"Do we have to worry about that now?"

The warning bells clanged in his head, but he closed his ears. "I suppose not."

She unbuttoned her blouse and let it fall to the floor. Her breasts were barely concealed by a lacy crimson bra. Against her pale skin, the color glowed like fire. "Last one in is a rotten egg," she said, smiling as she uttered the childhood taunt.

Something kicked in at that moment, some primeval urge to hunt and conquer. "Zoe," he warned. But it was too late. She had already disappeared into the bathroom. By the time he came to his senses and followed, she was completely naked, standing beneath the pelting water in the open shower. Droplets of water clung to her pert, pink nipples.

Though her actions indicated confidence, in her wary gaze he saw a diffident insecurity, as though even now she wasn't sure of his motives. Never taking his eyes off her, he stripped clumsily, stumbling against the counter when one leg of his pants caught on his shoe.

He stopped short of removing his boxers, because he was

far too close to an impatient climax. His hands fisted at his hips. He took deep, cleansing breaths, searching for control.

Zoe watched him intently, her golden hair darker now, the color of pale molasses. "You planning to stand there all night?" Again she taunted him. "I could use some help with the spots I can't reach."

To hell with control. He ripped his underwear down his legs and kicked it aside. Zoe's wide-eyed gaze settled on his penis and stayed there. He saw her swallow and lick her lips. "I'll wash spots you didn't even know you had," he threatened.

When he joined her in the shower, she backed against the far wall. Without asking, he took the soap from her lax grip and slid the sandalwood-scented bar from her throat to her navel.

Zoe's eyelids fluttered shut. Her lips parted and her respiration grew shallow. Now that he was in reach of what he wanted, he was able to gain a measure of delayed gratification. "Does that feel good?" he asked, pretending he was cool and calm. Inside his chest, his heart raced madly.

She stirred restlessly, one of her bare thighs brushing his. "Yes." The single syllable was slurred.

When he managed to move his gaze from her face to her breasts and onto the real estate below, he noticed the small fluff of feminine curls that had been trimmed in a tiny heart. He touched the shape with a single fingertip. "I like this, sweet Zoe. As far as I can tell, you collect hearts everywhere you go."

"Don't tease," she muttered, opening her eyes and gazing at him with such a beseeching look that for a single breathless second he would have given her anything she asked for.

He rotated his hand in the air. "Turn around. I'm not done."

Complying with just the right amount of sulky obedience, she flattened her hands against the wall of the shower and bowed her head. As he tucked her hair forward over her shoulder, Liam's heart bounced once and lodged uncomfortably in the vicinity of his throat. This was supposed to be a game. But looking at her like this swamped him with feelings that went beyond simple lust.

The nape of her neck struck him as painfully defenseless. Her shoulder blades were a tad too pronounced, but the line of her spine led to an ass that curved like a perfect, ripe peach.

Reaching for a washcloth, he lathered it and began to wash her back. If Zoe's little sighs and murmurs were any indication, she enjoyed his attention. Shortly, he abandoned the rag and used his bare hands to soap up her slick, creamy skin. His fingertips learned the dips and valleys of her body.

Unable to resist, he rested his erection in the cleft of her bottom, and pressed his lips to the top of her spine. "I don't know what I've done right in my life to deserve this moment, but I would walk through fire to have you again and again."

She lifted her head and glanced over her shoulder with a sultry smile that shot his blood pressure into the danger zone. "You haven't *had me* yet," she pointed out.

"Are you complaining? I thought women loved foreplay."

"I'm merely pointing out that you don't have to work so hard. I'm all yours, Liam."

Four simple words. Four teasing, erotic, knee-weakening syllables. *I'm all yours, Liam.* Did she really mean it? Did she have a clue how starved he was for her and only her, no matter the consequences?

His libido snapped the chains of his intellect. "Turn around, woman. Put your hands over your head."

Nine

When Zoe faced Liam, she realized in an instant that they had segued fast and hard from teasing flirtation to gut-deep lust. His pupils were dilated…. Only a tiny rim of royal blue remained. The dark flush on his cheekbones gave him the look of a warrior.

Shoulders that seemed impossibly wide bracketed a chest that was a miracle of nature. Muscle and sinew and a faint smattering of dark hair. The man who appeared so sophisticated and debonair in a tailored suit was a dominant male in his prime.

Oxygen evaporated, leaving her breathless and woozy. She could have blamed it on the hot water and the steamy air, but she had a clue it was more to do with the searing blue of Liam's eyes and the way he raked her from head to toe with a claiming stare.

Slowly, she lifted her arms until the backs of her hands rested against the ivory-colored marble wall veined in gold. "Take what you want," she said, wondering if she could push him beyond a civilized edge. Why it mattered so much to her, she couldn't say. Perhaps it hearkened back her earlier desire to know the Liam who existed behind the veil of courtly manners.

He vibrated with a hunger that was almost tangible. Deliberately, he caught each of her nipples between his thumbs and forefingers and tugged firmly. Fire shot from the sensitive flesh he tormented to the aching juncture of her thighs. Moisture bloomed in hidden places, moisture that had nothing to with the force of the shower and everything to do with Liam's touch.

Meeting his gaze at such close range became impossible. Her eyes downcast, she witnessed the fascinating swirl of his navel and the way his narrow hips gave way to powerful thighs. His erect shaft reared against his taut abdomen.

When he cupped her breasts with soapy hands, she jumped and moaned.

His forehead rested against hers. "You enchant me, lovely Zoe."

"I don't think I can stand much more of this," she said, with absolute sincerity. "I'm a heartbeat away from a world-class orgasm."

"Should I be flattered?" His husky voice teased her ear as he leaned into her and ran his hands up her arms so slowly she wanted to scream. When he reached her wrists, he gripped them tightly. Now his erection probed the soft flesh of her belly.

Her knees weakened to the point of collapse. She closed her eyes and whimpered.

Liam's response was instant. He kissed her hard. "Where did you go, Zoe? I want you here. With me."

Opening one eye, she managed a small grin. "Do you really want to know?"

His gaze sharpened as he absorbed her meaning. "God, yes. Tell me, wicked girl."

She dropped her head to the side, giving him better access to the sensitive spot beneath her ear. "I was imagining that you were a Viking marauder and I was your plunder."

Liam went perfectly still. Except for his thick shaft that twitched wildly. "Did you resist me, Zoe?"

She curled a leg around his hairy thigh, rubbing herself against him without shame. "I tried. But you smelled so good and you tasted like wine and decadence. I decided I had no choice but to cooperate."

The noise he made then was somewhere between a laugh and a curse. "I thought I was the one with Irish storytelling genes."

She flexed her fingers, testing the strength of the hands that manacled her wrists. "You inspire my imagination, Liam Kavanagh."

"Keep going. I'm intrigued." He kissed her temple and each of her eyelids. The delicate caresses were in direct opposition to the way his hips pinned her to the wall.

With her lower lip caught between her teeth, she pretended to ponder. "I suppose you could lift me and take me here and now, but it seems a mite dangerous with all this wet marble."

He bit her earlobe, sending a hot rush of blood to her core. "What other choice do we have?"

It was hard to form a coherent thought. But Liam appeared to be caught up in her little fiction, so she struggled for the image that would entertain him. "Your servants have prepared a bed for you. With velvet covers and silken sheets."

"Sounds comfy."

His wry comment forced her to stifle a giggle. Trying to stay in character was a challenge. "You are determined that I will obey you, so you stretch out on your back and force me to service you."

Liam scooped her into his arms with a rash intensity that threatened to dump them both on the shower floor. He grabbed for a towel and ran it carelessly over her breasts.

"Doesn't matter if we're wet," he said, his expression agitated. "Define *service*."

She linked her arms around his neck. "I have to taste your manly desire."

One dark eyebrow shot to his hairline. "Manly desire? Seriously?"

He deposited her on the bed and came down on top of her. "What happens next?"

"You're deviating from the plot." She shoved at his unyielding chest. "I'm supposed to be on top."

Rolling over onto his back, he wrapped a hand around his shaft. "I doubt that Vikings ever let women get on top."

"Not for actual sex, maybe. But surely if they wanted to get comfortable while the woman—"

"Tasted their manly desire?" His smile made her toes curl. "I'll do my best to cooperate."

Now that she had him where she wanted him, she almost lost her nerve. What did she know about satisfying a man like Liam? Her two sexual partners, both nice men, but not in Liam's league, had been quick off the mark and notably selfish.

Which was why she had decided to take a moratorium from physical interactions with the opposite sex.

But that high and mighty vow had evaporated when Bessie brought her to the Silver Beeches.

Shoving Liam's hand aside, she stretched out beside him on one elbow and stroked him from base to tip. "I'm pretty sure you promised to have me whipped if I don't give you pleasure."

A tiny drop of fluid leaked from the head of his erection. His voice sounded like gravel when he spoke. "I would never whip anyone as lovely as you. It would be a crime to mark that skin."

"Then maybe you threaten me with being chained in your dungeons."

"Vikings didn't have dungeons. They were always sailing on the high seas."

She sat up and glared at him. "Whose story is this, anyway?"

He waved a hand. His eyelids closed, and a smug smile lifted his lips. "Sorry, Scheherazade. Please continue."

She pinched his bicep, hard enough to bruise him if his muscles hadn't been so damned impressive. "No more talk from you." Though he pretended acquiescence, she knew that he could turn the tables at any moment. Deciding to take advantage of his momentary passivity, she bent over him and took him in her mouth.

"Sweet mother of God." Apparently her admonition about silence hadn't been taken seriously.

She licked him lazily, loving the way his hands clenched convulsively against the sheets when she let him feel the edge of her teeth. A feeling of feminine power mixed curiously with the yearning to bind him to her forever. Why did she have to be so tempted by something she could never have? She knew nothing of what it meant to build a home and a community, to be part of a tight-knit circle of love.

Most of her adult life had been spent in search of some elusive goal, an ephemeral vision of happiness. Now she could almost see the prize, but she had too many hurdles to cross before grasping it was possible.

Forcing back the negative emotions, she concentrated on giving Liam pleasure. His male body was so different from hers; lean and powerful and beautiful in a way that had inspired sculptors in ages past.

When she sensed she had pushed him too close to the edge, she drew back. "Did I please you, my Viking?"

Liam's chest heaved with the force of his labored breaths. If Zoe the chanteuse had brought him to his knees, then Zoe the Siren had finished him. He felt drugged, almost insensate with the exact pleasure she had described in her provocative tale.

It occurred to him that begging might not be his most manly option at this point, so he ground his teeth and sat up to stare at her. "Any more stories you want to tell?"

Her eyes rounded as if she sensed his imminent takeover. "No. Not really."

It appeared that she had forgotten her nudity. Earlier, in the shower, he had sensed her mild embarrassment at the way his eyes ate her up. But now, she was oblivious to the fact that her beautiful nakedness made him ache.

Without saying a word, he eased her onto her back. "Prepared to be ravaged, little captive." At the last moment, he remembered protection. Groaning at his complete lack of savoir faire, he dropped his head forward and put his hands on his thighs. "Condoms?" he muttered.

Zoe pointed. "In the vanity case. I hope they're not out of date."

He stumbled to the bathroom, took care of business and returned in record time.

Zoe lay exactly where he had left her, her arms outstretched above her head. Her hair had begun to dry in places. It was wavier now, giving her the look of a woman who had spent the last twenty-four hours in bed. She had one knee bent, with her foot planted against the mattress.

When she heard his footsteps on the carpet, she opened her eyes and smiled. "I've been waiting forever, Liam."

He stood beside the bed, his hand braced on the bedpost. Looking down at her fresh, pale-skinned body was almost enough. If he had been a poet, the sight of her would surely have inspired a sonnet. "The time for waiting is over." She had seduced him with song and then with her inventive imagination. "Tell me you want me, Zoe."

She arched her back, stretching from head to toe. "I do. I swear I do."

"Then we're both on the same page."

He eased down beside her and took his time with a tactile exploration. Her personality was so big, but her body was delicate of frame, more so since she had been ill. Laying his cheek on her belly, he played idly with the tuft of curls. Zoe inhaled sharply when his fingertip skated over a little bundle of nerves.

When he glanced up at her face, her eyes were squeezed shut and she had sunk her teeth into her bottom lip. Experimentally, he entered her with two fingers. The tight clasp of her body made him tremble. Soon, he was going to possess her. Completely.

Gently he used those same two fingers to simulate the act of lovemaking. With his thumb he brushed her clitoris repeatedly. Zoe quivered at his touch and came with a quiet sigh that indicated her satisfaction. At least he hoped so.

"There's more," he promised. Moving between her thighs, he fit the head of his erection at her entrance and pushed. Her passage gripped him in tight, moist heat as he slid all the way in. "Zoe," he groaned. "What have you done to me?"

She lifted her hips in invitation. "I might be able to go for round two. Just letting you know."

He chuckled hoarsely. "Always nice to get feedback." Humor in bed was a new one for him. But with Zoe, all the good things in life seemed to be rolled up in one beautiful package. Tenderness. Creativity. Laughter. Desire.

He moved in her deliberately, refusing to pick up the pace even when she wriggled beneath him and begged. The vision she made, lying beneath him with her face flushed in arousal, was a picture seared into his brain. He wanted to take her like this for hours. Every cell in his body was alive and humming with pleasure. He was hyperaware of his surroundings, all his senses on red alert.

The scent of their warm skin mingled with the fragrance of the freshly washed sheets. Zoe's limbs were sleek and strong as she curled her legs around his waist and clung to his shoulders.

The sounds she made as she came, not once but twice while he thrust repeatedly between her soft, firm thighs, were earthy, ragged…exhausted at the end.

The powerful surge of his impending climax left him breathless. He couldn't hold on, couldn't stretch the pleasure out one second longer. With a choked groan, his entire body shook in helpless release as he emptied himself until there was nothing left.

Zoe blinked as she tried to focus her reeling emotions. In a less ritzy hotel she might have found a water spot on the ceiling…something to latch onto while the universe cartwheeled around her.

Three orgasms in an hour? Sometimes she'd been lucky to have one. Liam Kavanagh possessed an impressive amount of knowledge about the female anatomy.

At the moment, he lay slumped on top of her, his body a heavy weight. That final go-round had short-circuited most of her synapses and left her feeling drunk and loopy with happiness.

She poked him in the back. "Are you still breathing?"

One male shoulder flinched as if to ward off a pesky fly. "No."

Since he couldn't see her face at the moment, she gave in to the urge to smile like a lovesick teenager. All her life she had searched for a place to belong, and turned out, it wasn't a place at all. It was a person.

The way Liam looked at her, even when they weren't in bed, made little bubbles fizz in her veins. She was pretty sure he saw her for who she really was. Not as an academic failure or an aimless wanderer, but a woman with worth and appeal. A woman who could make him laugh.

They might have skipped some steps in their budding *whatever-it-was,* but that could be remedied. She owed him a few explanations. After all, a relationship couldn't be built on evasions and half-truths.

Finally, Liam rolled onto his back, his chest still rising and falling more rapidly than normal. He sighed and stretched. "I think I entered another dimension."

Running her fingers along the nicely delineated muscles of his upper arm, she grimaced. "Don't lay it on too thick. I'm not *that* good."

He scooted onto his side and faced her, reclining on his elbow, head on his hand. "You're not good," he said. "You're incredible." With his hair rumpled and his chin covered in stubble, he looked like an invitation to sin.

Her face heated. Compliments were nice, but she didn't need flowery speeches. "I'm out of practice and underexperienced."

Liam tucked a stray lock of hair behind her ear, lingering to trace her bottom lip with his thumb. "I don't think that last one is a real word."

"You're awfully picky for a man who just—"

He put a hand over her mouth. "You mean for a Viking who enjoyed his barbaric spoils?"

"You make me sound like bad meat."

Liam laughed out loud, his expression far younger and more carefree than she had ever seen it. "I never know where your brain is going to go next."

She shoved him off balance and climbed on top, straddling his waist. "How's your recovery time? I know you're a lot older than me."

"Hey!" He scowled, but she could see the twitch of his lips. "Watch your step, little captive. I might consider spanking you after all."

She rested her hands on his chest. "Oooh, I'm so scared."

Something long and firm bumped up against her butt. Liam grinned. "Is that quick enough for you?"

Trying not to let him see that she was both impressed *and* aroused, she feigned indifference. "I suppose." She yawned theatrically. "As long as the main event isn't too quick."

He curled a hand behind her neck and dragged her down

to his chest until her mouth hovered over his. "This is the only way I know to shut you up."

The kiss was hard and warm and tender and insistent and passionate. It changed like a kaleidoscope, wooing her and winning her with every new variation. His tongue was slightly rough…and his apology gruff when his chin scraped hers.

At last she broke the connection and sat up, panting. "Is this where I'm supposed to take charge?"

Big hands clasped her waist and lifted her several inches, muscular arms flexing with impressive strength. "I'll get you started," he promised.

They both sighed when Liam lowered her onto his erection. The angle was new and tantalizing. Zoe rested her hands on his abdomen, her knees braced comfortably against the mattress. The sensation of being possessed, though she was in the dominant position, was inescapable.

Though Liam appeared to be relaxed, a flush of color had returned to his cheekbones. Inside her, his firm flesh moved impatiently with the slightest of motions.

Already, fresh ripples of sensation fluttered in Zoe's sex. Hoping her leg muscles had the endurance to please them both, she licked her lips and tucked her hair behind her ears. "Here we go."

Ten

Liam lost all track of time. When a woman like Zoe decided to take a man into her bed, the chosen male had no choice but to get down on his knees and thank the Almighty for the gift of such a fascinating, seductive woman. Only a fool would bypass this opportunity. Liam liked to think he was smarter than most men.

It wasn't just the sex. Though that was off-the-charts phenomenal. It was the fact that Zoe threw herself into lovemaking with an abandon and a giving nature that made her incredibly vulnerable.

How did she know that Liam wasn't only using her? Or maybe she didn't care. Maybe she was using him.

She was asleep now, her relaxed body draped over his like an exquisite throw. Her skin was hot and soft against his harder frame. As he winnowed his fingers through her hair, separating the silky strands, he inhaled the faint scent of her shampoo. In the aftermath of a physical cataclysm, his questions returned. Who was Zoe Chamberlain?

He told himself she had a right to her secrets, but now that he had tasted her essence and had learned the manner in which her body responded to his, he was obsessed with finding out more about her. Was he being taken in by a beautiful and accomplished con artist?

A few moments later when she stirred, he wasn't prepared for the way she looked at him. He'd expected a sleepy feminine smile, or a teasing suggestion that they start all over again. Instead, her expression was guarded…as if she expected him to do or say something that required armor on her part.

It struck him that she was right. His first impulse had been to ask his pointed questions while her defenses were down. Her startling ability to anticipate his responses so accurately both annoyed and shamed him. Was he *that* predictable? Disgruntled with himself and with her, he slid out of bed feigning a deliberately bland mood that hopefully disguised his turbulent emotions.

He picked up his boxers and pants. "I have an early conference call in the morning. I'll let you get your rest."

She sat up in bed, sheet tucked under her arms, and stared at him as he dressed. "Was it something I said?"

"What do you mean?" It irked him that her big-eyed solemnity made him feel guilty when he had nothing for which to apologize.

She nibbled her bottom lip, perhaps unconsciously. "I thought you might spend the night."

Pausing for a moment as he pretended to locate a renegade sock, he shook his head. "I have responsibilities. If no one can find me, they'll be worried."

"Well, heavens," she said, unmistakable hurt warring with indignation in her gaze. "What a tragedy that would be."

She was making fun of him. Again. As if dependability and steadfastness were traits to be mocked. Coming on the heels of what had been an incredible evening, her words stung more than they should have.

He shrugged into his shirt and fastened the buttons. "Not all of us have the luxury of flitting around the country wherever the wind takes us."

As soon as the words left his lips, he regretted them. "I'm sorry, Zoe," he said quickly. "That was low."

Sitting there like a courtesan dismissing an unwanted suitor, she shook her head, her smile bleak. "You're entitled to your opinion. I'm flighty and unfocused and selfish. God forbid that you should ever get out and have some fun. Is that what this is about? You took an evening off to go somewhere as bourgeois as a bar? You slept with me without analyzing the ramifications? Surely I must be leading you down the rosy path of destruction."

"Don't get carried away. I apologized."

"Yes, you did. But only for saying the words. Not for thinking them. I'd like you to leave now, please."

He took a step toward the bed, wondering why the hell he was dressed when all he wanted to do was crawl back beneath the covers with her.

Zoe stopped him with an upraised hand. "Go. Before I call the hotel owner and have you evicted. Oh, wait. That's you."

Crossing his arms over his chest, he glared at her. "Are you sure you aren't a natural redhead? That temper of yours is nasty."

"At least I *have* feelings," she said, her eyes shiny with what he hoped to God were not tears. "You stalk around your domain dressed to the nines and expecting everyone to dance to your tune. What a boring life that must be. I feel sorry for you."

A vein throbbed in his neck. The impulse to drag her to her feet and kiss her senseless was strong. But someone had to be a grown-up. "You've made your opinion very clear. Perhaps my brother is more your speed."

"Perhaps he is."

They were shouting at each other. Probably in danger of awakening everyone on the floor.

With a curse that came nowhere near expressing his mental state, he turned on his heel, dragged open the door, and despite his instincts to fling it shut with a crash, closed it carefully as he stepped into the hall.

Zoe cried herself to sleep. The next morning, puffy eyes and a splitting headache added to her general state of misery. Trapped by the breakdown of her automotive companion, she indulged in a much-deserved pity party.

Not that there was anyone around to offer sympathy. By midmorning she had run out of tears and patience. It was a beautiful day, and she was not going to let an uptight, play-by-the-rules jerk make her feel bad about herself. What he had going for him, though, was her memories of the way he had touched her so tenderly and yet with such hunger. As if he'd been starving for her and only her.

Well, that was that. She couldn't in all good conscience sleep with a man who thought so little of her. Her self-respect was important. If Liam didn't know how delightful it was to stop and smell the roses, then he didn't deserve her. Life was short. It deserved full participation or nothing at all.

In her travels she had seen the most magnificent natural scenery and the most bleak and disgusting of human situations. She had mingled with the elite of society and at other times shared soup with the down-and-outs who had little strength left to cling to the end of their ropes.

Though she had battled loneliness and fear from time to time, she had never lost her conviction that life was worth living and that the only way to grow and evolve as a human was to stretch your wings. She'd had some rough spots in her life. Everyone had. But she couldn't complain. Because she had never gone hungry, and she had never known true despair, though she had come close a time or two.

Liam had experienced rough spots as well. And like Zoe, he had adapted without complaining. But while Zoe was content to accept the world as it was, Liam's personality was more controlling. He was the kind of man who felt it necessary to take care of everyone and everything. He felt it was his duty to make sure the world turned on its axis as it should. Zoe was only interested in seeing the next sunrise. Perhaps she and Liam were simply too different to relate to each other.

When self-reflection and introspection palled, she rolled her eyes at her reflection in the mirror and showered rapidly, closing her mind and heart to images and memories of the last time she'd stood beneath the spray. Such self-indulgent reflections were counterproductive to her resolution to make the most of today.

Dressing in another version of the disguise she had worn into town previously, she made her way surreptitiously to the front of the hotel. Her heart beat rapidly, and her palms were sweaty. She wasn't sure which would be worse…seeing Liam or not seeing him.

By the time she had requested the loaner car and slid behind the wheel, it was clear that her host was engaged elsewhere in the hotel. Which was, of course, of no consequence to her.

Once again, she enjoyed the drive down the mountain. Springtime in western North Carolina was achingly beautiful. Mighty evergreens poked at the blue sky. Flowers blossomed everywhere. Birds flitted and sang their songs. Even without Liam, Bessie's choice of stopping places would get an A+ in Zoe's book. Despite the rocky start to her day, she appreciated the opportunity to continue roaming around the shops and spots of interest that comprised the heart of Silver Glen.

First off, she stopped by the Silver Chassis, only to be informed by an overly flirtatious teenager that the owner of the repair shop had driven to Asheville to pick up some parts, and that there was no progress to report about Bessie. The news didn't surprise her, but she had to fight an urge to sneak past the kid and take a look for herself.

After wandering for half an hour, she grabbed a soda and a hot dog from a fast food place disguised as a miniature chalet, and sat on a bench in the sun to eat it. The nature of her meal, compared to what she could have enjoyed had she not left the hotel, was amusing.

Food was not that big a deal to her. Which was why she could travel anywhere and everywhere with relatively little trouble. Deliberately choosing to live week to week with little in the way of material possessions was her own personal rebellion. The fact that her truculence might have had its day was an ever-growing source of concern and dismay.

She'd told herself for several years that she enjoyed her transient lifestyle, her gypsy itinerary. But the truth of the matter was, she was afraid to go home. She dreaded going back to the house where she had grown up. To start over again would mean facing her demons. A course of action that seemed not only depressing, but well nigh impossible.

Crumpling the paper sack that held the remains of her meal, she tossed it in a trash receptacle and stood to stretch. Once she returned to the hotel later this afternoon, perhaps she could make sure Liam was nowhere near the workout room, and she would be able to exercise in peace.

As she walked back toward her car, she glanced across the street at the Silver Dollar, its neon signs extinguished midday. The doors wouldn't open until four, but perhaps Dylan was around. She had a sudden urge to talk to the only other Kavanagh male she knew.

There was no doorbell, so she simply knocked and knocked until a rumpled Dylan answered, covering a yawn with his hand. He scrubbed a hand across his face. "I may have forgotten to mention that I'm not a morning person. If you want to sing here again, you might want to remember that."

She eased past him without an invitation. "Wow. Another grumpy Kavanagh man. Is it something genetic?"

Dylan wandered over to the bar and waved a hand. "You may as well have a seat since you're here." He grabbed a filter, put on a pot of coffee, and yawned again.

Zoe scooted up onto a stool and propped her elbows on the bar. "Rough night after Liam and I left?"

He poured himself a glass of water and downed a couple of aspirin. "Some of the guys stayed after I closed to play poker. It was close to three before they left, so I crashed on the sofa upstairs instead of driving home."

"Did you win?"

His wicked grin was much like his brother's. "I always win." He lifted a container of lemonade. "Want a drink?"

She nodded. "Might as well." It occurred to her that she might need an ally if she ever hoped to secure Liam's affections. Not that she was sure such a goal was admirable or even possible. But after last night, she'd probably be willing to give it a shot if the eldest Kavanagh weren't such a pain in the ass.

"Tell me," she said as she sipped her drink and studied the rather large painting of a nude reclining woman that hung over the bar. "Is it just me, or is your big brother an opinionated, judgmental, arrogant, overbearing pig?"

Dylan winced as he rubbed the spot between his eyebrows. "You should cut him some slack, Zoe."

"Why? I really want to know."

"Well, for one thing, he's a damned nice guy."

"Couldn't prove it by me."

"I guess he didn't take my advice."

"What advice?"

"Never mind," Dylan said quickly. "Let's get back to Liam. It's not really his fault he's so serious. When most sixteen-year-old kids were playing video games and going out for sports, my brother was taking a crash course in becoming the head of a big, loud, complicated family and running the business with Mom. All the rest of us had the luxury of doing whatever we wanted to with our lives. But Liam got stuck with the hotel."

"He claims he enjoys it."

"And he does, I'm sure. To a point. But he gave up a lot for us. So, if he occasionally has the annoying habit of thinking he's always right, it's probably because he is."

"I might have known you'd take his side. All you men stick together."

Dylan drained his first cup of black coffee and poured a second. Standing behind the bar, he looked as natural in his element as Liam did in his. "It might not be a bad idea, though, for you to coax him out of his office while you're here. Tell him you want to hike."

"Do I?"

"There are dozens of trails up and down and over the mountain. Several waterfalls, too."

Zoe felt her face flame and couldn't do a thing to stop it.

Dylan lifted an eyebrow. "I'm guessing he's already led you down the garden path?"

"Is that a euphemism?"

He gave her an innocent smile. "Not at all. The Silver Beeches gardens are legendary."

"I'll just bet they are," she muttered. Glancing at her watch, she grimaced. "I'd better get back. I want to work out in the gym before I eat another one of those calorie-laden dinners."

Dylan rinsed his cup and set it in the sink. Raking both hands through his hair, he shook his head. "You know that no one holds a gun to your head and makes you eat that crème brûlée."

Her stomach growled, no longer appeased by the hot dog. "I'm well aware of that. But I wouldn't want to hurt the chef's feelings."

"Whatever helps you sleep at night." He came out from behind the bar and paused to kiss her cheek before grabbing a broom. "You were a hit last night. Several of the guys were none too happy to see you going home with Liam."

"You're being kind."

He made her lift her feet, sweeping peanut shells into a pile. "Not at all. Anytime you want to do an encore performance, just ask. But in the meantime, try to forgive my brother for whatever dumb-ass thing he did. We men are clueless sometimes."

"I've noticed."

"And take my suggestion to heart. I'll bet you a hundred dollars that all you have to do is invite him to take you exploring and he'll shed that suit."

The image made her smile. "Is that what he is to you? Superman?"

"Damn straight. But I'll deny it to my grave if you tell him I said that. We like to keep him humble."

She hopped down from the stool and avoided the peanuts. "Thanks for the advice. What do I owe you for that and the lemonade?"

Dylan shook his head and yawned again, leaning against his broom. "It's on the house."

Returning to the Silver Beeches, Zoe was torn about whether or not she wanted to seek out her host or to avoid him entirely. As she swung around the final curve and slowed down to ease onto the flagstone apron in front of the hotel, the matter was settled for her. Liam stood on the top step, decked out in what looked to be an expensive hand-tailored suit and a crisp white shirt. It never failed to impress her that he managed to look so impeccably groomed every damn minute of the day.

Of course, there *had* been a few moments last night when she'd managed to rumple his sartorial perfection. The memories made her neck heat. For one second, she contemplated making a U-turn and beating a hasty retreat back down the mountain. But the venue was much too public for such a humiliating escape.

Instead, she put the car in Park, took a deep breath, and reminded herself that she was a woman of the world. Liam Kavanagh could not rattle her if she kept her cool. She wouldn't allow it.

His eyes narrowed as he watched her step out of the car. "I didn't see you in the dining room at lunch."

She handed the keys to the valet, shouldered her purse, and picked up the package she'd purchased after her talk with Dylan. "I've been out," she said airily.

As she climbed the shallow steps, Liam stared at her, his gaze intense. "Where?"

She stopped in front of him, one step down. He towered over her like a judge as he awaited her answer. "Does it matter?" she asked, trying not to notice how wonderful he smelled.

Guests milled around them, and the valet was still in earshot. "Of course not," Liam said, his voice stiff. "I was merely wondering if your day had been pleasant."

"Aren't you concerned about my nights, as well?"

Shock flared briefly in his eyes before his lids lowered and his jaw clenched. "Your nights are not my affair."

She brushed past him, running her free hand along his forearm as she walked by. "I'm hurt that you've abandoned me so easily," she whispered in his ear. "If you'd like to chat about it and regroup, I'll be in the parlor for high tea at four. Why don't you join me?"

Eleven

Liam didn't particularly like tea. Even so, he found his way to the parlor at 4:10 determined to let Zoe see that she wasn't calling the shots. To his dismay, once he finally entered the room, he saw her surrounded by a bevy of admirers. He decided not to fight the crowd, and instead, worked the room, conversing with guests and generally making sure his presence was known and appreciated.

In upscale hospitality, as in most things, the personal touch was what made a business stand out from the competition. Many of the people in this room were repeat bookings. Liam kept tabs on every aspect of the hotel's services, from the most mundane detail to the most outrageously expensive special request.

Though he had come to his mother's aid originally out of necessity, in the intervening years, he had discovered that he enjoyed making people feel at home in Silver Glen and welcome at the Silver Beeches Lodge. He wasn't the kind of man who would enjoy idle time spent on yachts or in casinos. This life at the Lodge had perhaps chosen him and not the other way around, but it was a good match for his set of skills, and it was different every day. He enjoyed the challenges.

Zoe met his gaze across the room at least twice before she finally dismissed her contingent and crooked a finger. It was a small matter of pride and control that Liam lingered a couple more minutes in another conversation before crossing the expensive carpet and stopping in front of the woman who was rapidly driving him out of his wits.

She patted the seat beside her. The particular item of furniture upon which she sat was an antique love seat with a carved wooden frame and plump, red-velvet upholstered cushions. Zoe reclined against the arm comfortably, one foot tucked beneath her. Her short and sassy madras skirt would have been more suited to the tropics, but on Zoe, it worked. The short-sleeved jersey knit T-shirt in a shade of teal that matched one of the stripes in the skirt was modest. But it clung to her breasts in a way that made it impossible for him to ignore her sexuality.

Sitting down beside her, he leaned back with a sigh. "I suppose you want to talk about last night."

She shook her head vehemently. "Not at all. I've never enjoyed rehashing my mistakes."

He winced. "Is that what it was? A mistake?" They were situated in a small island of intimacy, far enough away from the other occupants of the large room that they couldn't be overheard, but still on public display. The venue was guaranteed to keep his more reckless impulses under control. Probably.

Zoe picked at a loose thread on her skirt. "If it hadn't been a mistake, you would have stayed the night. It was pretty clear that you were having second thoughts. It's okay. I get it."

"I'm fairly certain you don't *get it*," he said, "because I'm pretty sure I don't even *get it*." He had regretted leaving her the moment he walked out her door last night. But there was enough confusion churning in his gut to stop him from going back and taking her over and over until morning…the way he wanted to. Wild abandon was not his M.O. Being around Zoe showed him facets of his personality he'd either deliberately buried or had never acknowledged at all.

She shot him a sideways glance from beneath thick, sooty lashes. Her blue eyes were one of her most beautiful features. Luminous and lovely, they by rights should have been windows into her soul. But Zoe was a pro at dissimulation. Though her bubbly personality appeared open and guileless, the truth was, she was secretive and kept her own counsel.

"I'm sorry I make you angry," she said quietly.

He ground his teeth. "I'm afraid for you."

"You don't have to be. I've been taking care of myself for a long time."

Both of her feet were now planted on the floor, her black ballet flats side by side. He wondered if the change in physical position meant she was prepared to run.

"You can trust me, Zoe."

"Is trust a prerequisite for crazy sex?"

"Most people would say so."

"I'm not most people," she pointed out with perfect truth.

"No, you're not. But I think you're in some kind of trouble, and if you and I are going to spend some time together, I'd prefer not to be blindsided. Especially if I might need to protect you."

At last a faint smile lifted the corner of her kissable lips. "Ah, the caveman thing. I love it. Though it's quite ridiculous, you know. I've been on my own for a long time."

"Okay, then. What if I just *want* to protect you? Would you agree to that? As long as I freely and fully admit that you don't have to have a man to look out for you?"

She patted his knee. Briefly. Decorously. "I can live with that. As long as you promise you won't protest or resist me if and when I try to get you to lighten up."

"Does that mean what I think it means?"

"In your dreams."

He loved sparring with her. The quick banter with its sexual overtones stimulated him both physically and mentally. No other woman of his acquaintance spoke to him the way Zoe did. Except for his mother—who had the ability to take him down a notch or two when the occasion warranted—most people, both male and female, either kowtowed to him, or at the very least treated him with deference.

Not that he expected or demanded such a thing. In fact, it often irritated him that his money and position caused people to treat him as some kind of exalted being. No danger of that with Zoe. Perhaps that was what drew him so strongly into her orbit. The childlike innocence of her outlook on life and the way she related to him simply as a man was refreshing and deeply appealing.

"Is this what you call regrouping?" he asked, hearkening back to her invitation to tea.

She leaned forward and picked up a china cup, lifting it to her lips. As she sipped delicately, she eyed him over the rim. "I bought hiking boots today."

The odd segue caught him off guard. "You did?"

"For a man who is disgustingly wealthy, you work too hard."

"Is there a question in there somewhere? And besides, working hard is not a crime."

"Most people with your bank balance would be traveling the world."

He shrugged. "Plenty of time for that."

She carefully returned the cup to its saucer and snagged a small cookie. "You can't bear the thought that all this could toddle along just fine without you."

Her comment was uncomfortably close to the mark. If the hotel and his mother no longer needed him, he would be adrift in a sea of uncertainty. "No one is indispensable. But I like to think that what I do is important."

"Of course it is. But you need balance, my friend."

"That's not the first time you've alluded to our being friends. I'm honored…I think." He grinned at her. The residue of powdered sugar on her bottom lip made him desperate to lick it away, but he and Zoe were surrounded by interested eyes.

Her exuberant smile dimmed. "I don't have close friends. Tons of acquaintances on at least three continents, but not the kind of people I can call at three in the morning. That's the downside of always being on the move, I suppose."

Again, he glimpsed a deep vein of vulnerability. A woman like Zoe was alone only by choice. What in her past had prompted the vagabond lifestyle? The only way he was going to get answers was to spend time with her. That would be no hardship. And in doing so, he could prove to her that he knew how to kick back and have fun.

"You mentioned boots," he said.

"*Hiking* boots. You'll be impressed."

"I'm guessing this is where I'm supposed to offer my services as a guide?"

Her smile was innocent. The expression in her eyes was not. "That would be lovely…if you're not too busy."

He recognized the challenge for what it was. "I think I can make time for you." The prospect was damned appealing. Spring in the mountains was his favorite time of year. "How about tomorrow morning? Nine o'clock. Meet me in the lobby…I'll ask the chef to pack us a picnic."

Her delighted smile bathed him in sunshine and warmth. "I can't wait."

Zoe felt a definite pang moments later as she watched him walk away. This game she played, pushing him to see if he would go along with her mischief, was dizzyingly fun. As she dabbed her lips with a crisp damask napkin and prepared to rise, a woman appeared at her elbow. "Ms. Chamberlain. Lovely to see you. Do you mind if we chat for a moment?"

Liam's mother wore a navy dress that complemented her coloring and suited her air of dignity.

The sinking feeling in the pit of Zoe's stomach felt much like the time she had been summoned to the principal's office for cutting her best friend's hair without permission. "Of course," she said, waving a hand. "Please join me."

Maeve summoned a waiter for a fresh pot of tea and waited as he poured each of them a cup. Zoe had drunk so much by this time that she could have floated away. But she wasn't about to refuse an overture from the Kavanagh matriarch.

When the formalities were complete, Maeve sat back and eyed Zoe with a faint smile. "I notice that my son is spending a fair amount of his time with you."

"He's an attentive host," Zoe replied, the words matter-of-fact. Surely Maeve couldn't know what had happened in Zoe's room. "And your son, Dylan, has been kind enough to let me sing at the Silver Dollar." She was hoping to steer the subject into less volatile territory. Discussing one's lover with the lover's mother was more than a little awkward.

Maeve set her cup on the low table in front of them. "I am a firm believer in innocent until proven guilty."

Zoe gulped inwardly. "I don't follow."

"It's simple." Maeve shrugged. "You are an unconventional woman. And some of the details of your life have raised questions with my son, as you know. But you are a guest in my hotel, and as such will be afforded the utmost courtesy. I do, however, have one gentle warning."

"Yes, ma'am?"

The respectful address did nothing to alleviate Maeve's somber expression. Her gaze pinned Zoe's without apology. "Don't screw with my son's emotions, or I'll have to intervene." The words were crisp and unequivocal. "He's a grown man. But men can be blinded by their physical needs. If you are what you seem to be...a nice girl with a penchant for traveling lightly and often, then so be it. But if you have any notion of manipulating my son for your own personal or financial gain, I *will* send you packing."

It was possible Zoe's mouth gaped. She wasn't accustomed to such blunt speaking, nor such evidence of a parent's love and determination. Some women would be highly offended by Maeve's speech. Zoe, however, couldn't help but think how lucky Liam was to have such a force of nature guarding his back.

She swallowed the rush of envy and yearning. Maeve would be an awesome mother-in-law. The thought brought her up short. Where had that come from? "I swear you have nothing to fear from me, Mrs. Kavanagh. I'm only passing through. Your son is a wonderful man, but we have little in common."

"Because you see Liam as staid and serious?"

"I wouldn't have said *staid*." More like sexy as hell.

"It might help if I tell you a bit of the Kavanagh story," Maeve said. "Do you have a few moments?"

"Of course."

Maeve poured herself another cup of tea and selected a macaroon from the plate of delicacies. Taking a bite, she put it on the saucer with her teacup and grimaced. "Living in a hotel with a world-renowned chef is a terrible strain on my willpower."

"You're an attractive woman. I can't see any extra pounds."

"Dear girl." Now Maeve had a twinkle in her eye. "No wonder my son is smitten with you."

That didn't seem to require an answer. Zoe pretended to sip her zillionth cup of tea, beginning to feel like a character in a period drama, minus the cool clothes.

Dylan's mother sighed, her expression reflective. "The original Kavanaghs came to this country in the 1920s. Times were hard, and this rocky, mountainous land was all they could afford. Our Kavanagh story and indeed our whole family might have died out long ago except for the fact that at the height of the Great Depression, an ancestor discovered a thick vein of silver hidden deep in a cave somewhere here on the mountain."

"Sounds like a fairy tale."

"It does, doesn't it? That one event swung the tide, and from then on, the family fortunes prospered. Though a landslide eventually obscured the mine, there was enough money and sufficient sound investments to keep marching forward."

"Had the mine been tapped out?"

"No one really remembers. But my late husband, Reggie, was convinced that he had to locate it. Unfortunately, he was egged on by a woman who came over from Ireland claiming to be a distant cousin. She said she was writing the Kavanagh family history, and we had no reason to believe otherwise." Maeve's expression for a moment reflected pain. "The woman was quite lovely, and I'm sorry to say that my husband was very weak. They began an affair."

Zoe's heart broke for Liam's mother. "I'm so sorry."

Maeve shrugged, her lips twisting. "Even Liam was infatuated with her. Until he realized what was going on. Then he hated her. Once she and Reggie were sleeping together, she became even more insistent that it was possible to find the mine. Reggie believed her because her certainty fed his own fantasies of reopening the mine. It became an ugly obsession. One winter day when Liam was in high school, Reggie took off on one of his jaunts and never returned."

"And the woman?"

"She went back to Ireland. I had her investigated eventually. She lives in a low-rent flat in Dublin and works as a bank teller. I'm sure she was hoping that the American Kavanaghs would be her ticket out of a boring life."

"That's terrible."

"It was a long time ago. But a disappearance is not a clean break like a death. There are always questions. And of course, there was no possibility of my finding anyone else to love. By the time the requisite years had passed for Reggie to be declared legally dead, my children and the hotel had become my life."

"I can tell from what Liam says that you're a close-knit family."

"Yes. Liam and I even more so, because we work so closely together. He grew from a scared, angry teenager into a capable, caring man. But losing his father like that marked him. Though I never encouraged it, Liam was convinced he had no choice but to step up and be the head of the family. He was determined to be the antithesis of his father."

"How so?"

"Reggie was a wonderful, outgoing, loving man. But he was unable to see that his obsession with finding the mine was terribly selfish. The tragedy of his presumed death took something from my sons that I could never give back to them. I did my best to play the role of both parents, but a boy of any age needs his father. Because of Reggie's blindness, he robbed his children and did them a grave disservice. He had a responsibility as a dad, but he abdicated that obligation in favor of pursuing a fantasy."

"And now Liam is the exact opposite."

"In many ways, yes. I appreciate his dedication, and in fact, as a young man, he sacrificed much for me and for his family as a whole. I've prayed that he won't grow to resent me, but still sometimes I worry."

"Liam loves what he does. And he loves you." Zoe said the words with absolute conviction. And was rewarded by the look of gratitude in Maeve's damp eyes.

"Thank you for that," the older woman said. "I'm so close to the situation, it's difficult to be impartial."

"I think you're worried about nothing. I've seen men who resent their lot in life, and Liam isn't one of them."

"Tell me about your family, Zoe."

The sudden question, commonplace though it was, took Zoe completely off guard. She stuttered and buried her face in her teacup, taking a long gulp as she tried to regain her composure. It was one thing to analyze the Kavanagh family. Another again to delve into Zoe's past and present. Her kin were neither as charming nor as caring as Liam's. And Zoe had no real desire to reveal the skeletons in her closet.

When she thought she could speak without sounding defensive, she smiled. "My parents live in the northeast. Sadly, we're not very close."

"You're an only child?"

"Yes, ma'am."

Maeve shook her head, her expression exasperated. "Quit *ma'am-ing* me, if you please. It's unnecessary. Call me Maeve."

"I'd be honored."

"You know, Zoe…" She paused, her shoulders lifting and falling. "I don't have any daughters, only sons. But I think you are an extraordinary young woman, and I'd like to know you better."

Danger, danger, danger. If Zoe became too entwined in the life of the Kavanagh family, she might find it even harder to leave. And she always left eventually. Always.

Nevertheless, Maeve was waiting for an answer. "I'd like that, too," Zoe said, feeling the truth of the words in her heart. "And you don't have to worry. I'm not a threat to your son."

Twelve

The following morning when Liam watched Zoe step out of the elevator, his heart jolted. As she sauntered across the lobby to meet him, he realized he was in danger of doing something—or maybe even a few somethings—that was either irrational or stupid or wildly impetuous. The urge and the recognition of that urge alarmed him. He was not that kind of man.

Every set of male eyes in the vicinity tracked Zoe's progress. She wore her brand-new boots with the scrunched tops of big socks visible. But it was the miles of long, slim legs and the abbreviated khaki shorts that walloped him with a punch of lust and longing.

Every teenage boy in America had seen legs like those in naughty magazines hidden beneath mattresses.

When Liam finally dragged his gaze upward, the view was equally stunning. Zoe wore a plaid button-down shirt with the sleeves rolled to her elbows and the tails tied in a jaunty knot at her waist, exposing a shallow, sexy belly button.

Her golden hair was caught back in a ponytail. She lifted her hand and donned a pair of large tortoiseshell sunglasses, effectively shielding her gaze. "Good morning, Liam. Are we ready to go?"

It was a good thing he was standing behind the front desk. He needed a moment to capture his equilibrium. His throat dry as dust, he managed a smile. "I am. Did you use sunscreen?"

She nodded. "Top to bottom and everywhere in between."

Now there was an image. One he couldn't dwell on at the moment. "Good." His conversational expertise had been reduced to single syllables. Without further ado, he ushered her outside where one of his employees had brought around Liam's Jag.

Zoe patted the hood ornament as she walked around to the passenger side. "Promise not to bite me."

He wasn't sure if she was talking to the chrome cat or to him. If it was the latter, she was out of luck. Once the picnic basket was safely stowed in the backseat, he glanced at his companion. "All set?"

She nodded, her smile cheeky. "Bring it on."

The next half hour was the most fun he'd had in a long time…if you didn't count that night in Zoe's bed. He sent the Jag whizzing around curvy mountain roads, hanging just above the speed limit, but plenty fast enough to make Zoe shriek and laugh out loud.

Her enthusiasm and joy were contagious. The cloud-dotted sky was as perfectly blue as a brand-new crayon, full of pictures and dreams waiting to be summoned. The day was warm, but not miserably hot, the breeze a soothing balance for the sun's intensity.

Liam drove with one hand on the wheel, his left arm resting on the door. "I thought I'd take you to Rooster's Rest."

"How quaint. Sounds high."

He glanced deliberately at her bare legs. "You can make it."

For a moment, she took off her sunglasses and stared at

him. Though he dared not take his gaze off the serpentine road for longer than a split second, one look in her direction registered the awareness that hovered between them. His sex tightened uncomfortably, and his breathing quickened. Today's outing was all well and good, but he planned on persuading her to join him in a far more private, much more luxurious rendezvous. Very soon.

When they reached the pull-off that accessed the trail he had in mind, Zoe hopped out of the car and stretched. East of them and far below, the town of Silver Glen seemed to slumber in the sunshine. Zoe practically bounced on her toes. "Come on, slowpoke," she said.

Liam removed their lunch and raised the top of the car. The small picnic basket was fitted with two straps that slipped over the shoulders like a backpack. He donned it, adjusted the fit, and pointed. "Okay, Miss Impatience. Let's see what you've got."

In truth, Zoe had serious doubts about her ability to keep up with Liam. When wearing a dress suit he cut a formidable figure. But today, in professional-looking gear that had probably cost a fortune, he looked like a cover model for *Backpacker Magazine.* Broad shoulders...muscular calves and thighs. Boots that had the wear on them of a serious hiker.

His vented dark-green shirt hung loose over khaki shorts. In this environment, he was the ultimate male. Capable of conquering the wilderness and killing a bear with his two hands.

Okay, so maybe that last part was one part Daniel Boone legend and one part prehistoric female admiration, but wow...Liam Kavanagh was one hunky guy.

Though she suspected he was attempting to shorten his stride, she was breathless in half a mile. "Stop," she said, bending at the waist and trying to inhale oxygen. "Your legs are longer than mine."

"Sorry."

He didn't look sorry at all. In fact, he looked distinctly *something*. She couldn't quite put her finger on it. "What's wrong with you?"

His jaw tightened. "Nothing."

"Liar."

His sudden move startled her. Without warning he had her up against a tree, his hips wedged against hers. *"This* is what's wrong with me,*"* he said. His breath was hot on her cheek, the glaze of passion in his eyes unmistakable.

Rough bark pressed uncomfortably into her back, but she wouldn't have moved for anything. "Did you leave your polished manners back at the hotel along with your Italian-made suit?"

Finally, his monumental self-control snapped. "Damn you," he groaned. Like a man desperate for a lifeline, he took her mouth in a possessive kiss.

Her legs weakened as his voracious hunger devoured her. This was the reaction she'd been seeking, but the reality was far more intense than she had expected. Pulling away from her only long enough to dump the picnic basket on the ground, he was back in a half second, capturing her head in two big hands and tilting her mouth to his so he could slide his tongue between her lips and stroke the inside of her mouth.

Breathing was not all that important, she decided hazily. Her fingers clenched in his hair. "Please tell me you have condoms."

His answer was a muffled grunt that could have meant anything or nothing. She flinched when one of his hands slid beneath her shirt and shoved her bra aside to play with a taut nipple.

"Seriously, Liam," she said. "Do you?" They were rapidly reaching a point of no return. Her body was so primed, she would probably be embarrassingly quick off the mark the moment he entered her.

Rearing back to look at her, he inhaled sharply. "You

drive me insane," he said, his brow creased as if in confusion. "We're supposed to be exploring the great outdoors."

At that very moment, laughter and conversation reached them only seconds ahead of a large group of college-aged kids striding up the trail. There was barely time enough for Zoe to adjust her blouse and for Liam to take two quick steps backward.

The group was boisterous, calling out greetings and joking comments and jostling for position. In a few moments, the cluster of hikers disappeared around a bend up ahead.

Liam squeezed the bridge of his nose between his eyes. "Good Lord."

"Do you think they caught on?"

He lifted an eyebrow. "Oh, yeah."

"What do we do now? I don't want to run into them again. It would be too embarrassing."

"I hate to waste those new boots."

"They'll keep for another day."

"In that case, let's go someplace quiet and private for our picnic."

Zoe straightened from the tree, assuming her legs could now hold her up. "What a lovely idea, Mr. Kavanagh. I'm in your hands."

"Not yet, but we're getting there."

Liam drove with purpose, eager to reach their destination. The spot was farther away than he had planned to go, but minus the hike, they had plenty of time. He glanced sideways at his passenger who was being unusually quiet. "You okay?"

She nodded, her expression pensive. "Yes. Just enjoying the day."

He wished he knew what she was thinking, but women were complicated creatures, and Zoe more so than most. It wasn't conceit to say he could have taken her up against the tree back there. Zoe had been every bit as into the moment as he had been. Now, however, she seemed a million miles away.

At last, he spotted the sign he was looking for.

She perked up when he turned off the highway. "What's this?" she asked.

"A good friend of mine owns a series of rustic cabins that he rents out only in the summer months. I have a standing invitation to use them off-season, complete with a key. There's no electricity, but on a day like today, we won't need it."

A few hundred yards up a gravel road he had to unlock a gate. After driving the Jag past the metal swing bar, he relocked the barrier. The cabins came into view around the next bend.

Zoe got out of the car and examined the buildings. "These are cute," she exclaimed. Her shirt had rucked up, exposing a smooth pale abdomen.

Liam's fingers clenched around his keys, hard enough to leave marks in his palm. He had to get ahold of himself. But Zoe's innocent sexuality hit him hard, making him ache to have her. Pointing to the closest of the one-room structures as he put up the convertible top, he said, "The porch is covered. How about we sit over there to eat?"

She nodded. "Perfect."

There was no outdoor furniture, but between them they managed to spread a square damask cloth on the floor of the porch. The chef had done himself proud. Fresh salmon drizzled with a light sauce, a broccoli salad, sourdough bread, and apple-caramel cake for dessert.

Liam had added a bottle of expensive champagne. He popped the cork, filled two flutes, and handed one to Zoe.

They sat on the edge of the porch, their legs dangling, and consumed an impressive amount of food in short order. He was glad to see that Zoe had a good appetite. She needed a few extra pounds to satisfy him that she was truly recovered.

Though he knew the risk he was taking, he counted on the meal and the champagne to mellow her. "Will you tell me about your parents?" he asked quietly. "I would never betray your confidence." But if he went any farther with this relationship, there couldn't be secrets between them.

She didn't look at him, but he saw the way her jaw tightened. Resting one arm on an upraised knee, she sipped from a crystal flute, as comfortable as any princess at court.

When she finally spoke, her gaze was trained somewhere off in the distance. "I know I can trust you. I wouldn't have slept with you otherwise, but there's not much to tell. My mother is a wraith of a woman who has no opinions or interests other than the ones my father approves."

"Is he abusive?" It was a legitimate question and one he needed answered.

"It depends on how you define that word. Emotionally? Yes. He's very controlling."

"So you butted heads when he realized you weren't likely to let yourself *be* controlled."

"Very good. Go to the head of the class. When I left college, he was furious, but I was halfway around the world, so there wasn't much he could do about it. After my stint in the Peace Corps, I continued to travel. I've waitressed in Rome, taught English in South America and done laundry in Thailand. Whatever it took to fund my adventures."

"You're very resourceful." He couldn't help wondering how the platinum credit card and the money in her van fit into her explanation. "What was it like when you came home?"

"My father thought the ball was finally in his court. I made the mistake of moving back into the house, because I had really missed my mother, and I felt guilty about leaving her under my father's thumb unprotected."

"Then what happened?"

"He began to pressure me into going to work for him. Having a child like me instead of the son he wanted was always a great disappointment in his eyes, but I suppose it finally dawned on him that his only offspring was better than nothing."

"It must have been nice to know your father wanted you."

She looked straight at him for the first time, and he was appalled by the bleak sorrow in her gaze. For one brief second he caught a glimpse of another Zoe. The woman who carried secrets and hurts hidden from the world. "No." The negative was flat, no intonation. A statement of fact.

"What is his business?"

"Corporate greed. Crush the competition. Even without the specter of being under my father's domination, it was not a world I ever wanted."

"And he didn't take that well."

"Oh, no. Not at all. Things became unbearable in the house. My mother was caught in the middle, and the tension made her physically ill. I used to resent her for not standing up to him, but as I grew up, I finally understood that she is incapable of that. She had a wretched childhood. My father was her ticket out of a dreadful home environment. And he's been her security ever since."

"So what did you do?"

"I left. Again. That's when I started my music career, if you can call it that. There were still plenty of places in the good ole U.S.A. that I hadn't seen, so I went where the wind and the work took me."

"Is it lonely?" He genuinely wanted to know.

She shrugged. "Being human is to be lonely. It's a rare gift in life to find the person who completes you. Let's just say that the good outweighed the bad. My mother and I still communicate. I bought her an iPhone she keeps hidden from my dad. We call and text when he's out of town."

"I'm sorry, Zoe."

"I tried once more. I don't want you to think I'm as stubborn as my father. This past Christmas, my mom begged me to come home for the holidays. I was feeling blue and orphaned, so I did."

"And?" Her story riveted him.

"At first I thought we were mending fences. My father was on his best behavior. My mother actually glowed. There were parties and dinners, most of them business related, but still. On Christmas Eve, Dad called me into his office. I was expecting maybe a hug or a word of thanks for making my mother happy."

Liam saw the muscles in her throat work as she swallowed. A great ball of dread gathered in his chest, but he had asked the questions and now he had no recourse but to hear the tale to the end.

"That wasn't it?'

Her lips twisted in a cynical grimace so unlike the Zoe he knew that it gave him a pain in his chest. "He backhanded me across the face. Hard. I was so shocked I didn't know what to do. But he did all the talking. He told me he was sick to death of my immaturity and selfishness. That it was time to grow up and quit hiding behind my suitcase."

Liam's chest heaved. He wanted to say something, but the wrong words could hurt her, and he would slice his own wrists before he would do that. "Go on," he said softly.

"He told me that he had a friend on the police force. If I didn't cooperate with my father, I would be accused of stealing money from the safe in Dad's office. I would be arrested and taken to jail."

"Goddammit." Fury mixed with incredulity choked Liam and made it hard to breathe. Hard on the heels of that reaction was the sick realization that Zoe's van was stashed with money. Lots of money.

She had disappeared into some bad place, barely seeming to know he was there. "It was Christmas Eve," she said dully, as if he might have forgotten that fact. "I slipped upstairs and tried to explain to Mama why I couldn't stay. But I didn't tell her about his threat. I couldn't. She cried so hard it ripped my heart in two. While my father was on the phone, I packed a small bag and slipped out the back of the house."

"He didn't try to stop you or come after you?"

"No. Not at first. But sometime in early March I began to get the feeling I was being followed. I would see someone in the audience watching me, someone who looked out of place. I'd have to slip away under cover of darkness. Again. And again."

"It could have been your imagination." He was trying to convince himself that her story wasn't as awful as it sounded. But then he remembered the mysterious man Pierre had intercepted. The man looking for Zoe.

She shook her head. "Last week in Asheville I saw the same man. Twice. On the street. Following me on foot. That's when I hit the road again and ended up in Silver Glen."

"So the man who showed up here and talked to Pierre was probably the same fellow?"

"That would be my guess. And he'll come back again. So I won't be able to stay the whole six weeks. I can't go back home and be arrested. And I can't put your family through an ugly situation or a confrontation."

"That's why you asked Gary to paint your van. Even though it didn't need a paint job."

Shock lifted her eyebrows. "You and this Gary fellow must be bosom buddies. Remind me to pick another mechanic the next time."

There was a bite in her words, one he deserved. "I'm sorry."

"It doesn't really matter now, does it?" She drained her champagne, her expression for once so inscrutable he had no clue what she was thinking.

She curled her knees to her chest in a defensive posture, her arms linked around them. "If you brought me here to fool around, we've definitely killed the mood now, haven't we?"

Thirteen

Zoe felt like a punctured balloon. Again, like the hospital experience weeks ago, she experienced the notion that life was using her for a punching bag. This day had begun with such effervescence and simple joy that it was particularly painful to be dragged to a place she'd tried so hard to escape.

She understood Liam's questions. He was trying to understand her. The trouble was, she barely understood herself. But she cared about Liam, and for the first time in a long time, she wanted to let someone in.

Rising to her feet with one fluid motion, she brushed crumbs off her hands. "I'm going to wander into those trees over there for a private moment."

"Watch out for snakes."

Her nose wrinkled. His admonition wasn't a joke. That's all she needed. A snakebite on her lady parts.

After relieving herself and straightening her clothing, she wandered through the little grove of hardwood trees, enjoying the beauty of the somnolent afternoon. Perhaps she could stay here forever, hiding out from her father like a paranoid survivalist. The Unabomber had managed it for a long time. But Montana and North Carolina weren't exactly the same.

Despite having no concrete proof, she was very afraid that she was still being followed. Even though Pierre had done his best to hide her existence in the hotel, and even though she had told herself the danger was past, in her gut she knew it would never be over. Not until she put a stop to it once and for all. It would only be a matter of time before the mysterious man understood that he had been duped. He would come back, because the man paying him would never give up.

When would her father learn that she would not accept being under his domination the way her mother was? If Zoe could have rescued her mother, she would have. But she knew in her heart that her mom would never leave.

As she walked back over to the cabin, her heart began to splinter into a million little pieces. Liam waited for her. He stood with one hand braced on a support timber, his stance casual, but his gaze watchful.

She had to leave Silver Glen. It had been stupid and naive to think she could actually stay six weeks. She knew better than to let anyone get close to her, but Liam had slipped beneath her defenses. There was no future for them. But dear God, she loved being here in North Carolina with him. She loved the town and the hotel and sense of community and singing at the Silver Dollar, but most of all, she knew she could love Liam. If she allowed herself. But she wouldn't. She couldn't.

The only way she had been able to survive her nomadic lifestyle was to enjoy the people she met along the way, but never to fall into the trap of thinking they were family. She had a mother she loved very much, but her father had separated them. Imagining a dream in which Liam's family *became* her family was pathetic.

He liked her. And he desired her. That much was clear.

But Zoe lived on the road and Liam was rooted in Silver Glen. Permanently.

She didn't climb the stone steps to the porch. Instead, she shaded her eyes and stared up at him. Her sunglasses were in the car. "Do you mind if we go back now?" she asked.

Liam was torn. And deeply concerned about his own judgment. Was he allowing his sexual attraction to Zoe to blind him to the truth? In the minutes when she had left him briefly, he had pondered the existence of the money. Hidden in a panel of her van. An enormous amount of money. Enough for a man to hire an investigator to retrieve it. Did she plan to use it to pay her credit card bill?

Forcing himself to take a mental step backward, he asked a silent, hard-edged question. Could Zoe possibly be a manipulative con? Had she spun Liam this story in order to cover her tracks so that when her father caught up with her, Liam would take her side?

His mind shut down, refusing to deal with such an ugly supposition. The notion was repugnant in every way. Despite the growing mountain of evidence that said Zoe had secrets galore, and despite the experience in his youth that told him women could be devious, he trusted Zoe. Was he making the same mistake twice?

She stood, waiting for his answer. "Sure," he said. "But if you're up for it, we could climb to the top of this hill. There's a beautiful lake on the other side."

He watched her visibly hesitate and wished he could appease whatever demons she was battling. "I suppose it couldn't hurt."

Liam jumped off the porch and touched her arm. "I have an idea." He indicated for her to follow him, and they began walking around the cabin and up the grassy hillside behind. He matched his pace to hers and then gave voice to what was becoming an irresistible notion. "I have to go to New York tomorrow," he said. "I'm speaking to a consortium of high-end hotel owners about hospitality in the twenty-first century. I'd like you to go with me."

Zoe trudged beside him, head down. "Why?"

He sighed. "Nothing is ever easy with you, is it? Can't it be enough that I want to spend time with you?"

"How long would we be gone?"

"Three days."

"And what about my room at the hotel?"

"Which hotel?"

She stopped and struggled to catch her breath. The hill wasn't all that high, but it was steep. "I meant the Silver Beeches, but I suppose the question stands for both."

"We'll simply put your room at my hotel on hold. And in New York, it's up to you. One room or two."

"I don't want to fall in love with you, Liam."

The shock of her words knocked him back half a step. He ran a hand across the back of his neck. "I don't know how to answer that. And besides, I don't think you're in much danger. According to someone I know, I'm bossy and uptight and judgmental and I have a king complex."

"Don't forget arrogant."

He held out his hands. "See? You have nothing to worry about."

They continued walking, but his mind was not on the magnificent scenery. Had Zoe been expecting some sort of reciprocal response on his part after she made her veiled statement about having feelings for him? Had he hurt her by remaining silent? And did he want her to love him? Did he want to love her?

The questions threatened to drive him mad. That and the memory of thousands of dollars hidden away in her van. As a teenager he had watched his father be seduced by a woman with secrets. Liam had been infatuated with her as well. When her true colors were revealed, his entire family had been crushed, and his father was dead.

Liam was no longer an impressionable youth. But love could make a man blind.

At the crest, they stopped, joined in mutual accord by their admiration of the view. A small lake in the distance glittered, its surface silvered by the sun. "Have you ever sailed?" he asked her, searching for topics that weren't booby-trapped.

"Some. While I was in France. I made friends with sisters whose father was Comte something or another. They would take me home with them on the weekends and we would do all sorts of crazy things."

"Do you still hear from them?"

"No. We lost touch." She left it at that, so he didn't push.

A rumble of thunder sounded in the distance. The fluffy white "sheep" clouds that dotted the sky earlier in the day had morphed into angry, gray, roiling masses. "Better head back," he said. "We don't want to be trapped up here when it hits."

Their luck ran out halfway back to the cabin. The sky let loose with a deluge as if someone had opened a huge zipper overhead. In seconds, they were both drenched. Lightning danced around them and thunder roared. Liam cursed himself for not paying closer attention to the change in weather. Running now, they hurtled down the last incline.

A few hundred feet from the cabin, Zoe's heel skidded on wet grass, and she went down hard, tumbling twice before he could get to her. In other circumstances, her appearance might have been amusing, covered as she was in mud and grass, but he was too worried to pay much attention.

He scooped her into his arms, and with a stride that was long but steady, carried her the last few yards to the cabin. The only entrance was through the front door. He kicked it open. Musty air met them, the inside of the place cheerless and dark. Tiny rodents ran for the cover of darkness.

Zoe clung to his neck. "I'm not touching anything."

"Only for a second." He eased her down onto one foot

while he reached for a straight-backed chair that appeared to be fairly clean. Sitting down, he settled her in his lap. "How badly are you hurt?"

"Mostly just my pride. Though my ankle may be sprained and I think my hand is bleeding where I landed. Can't we go back to the hotel? I could sit on a jacket or towel or something so I don't mess up your car."

A thunderous boom made them both jump in sync. "Screw the car," he said forcefully. "We need to get you to a doctor. But it's too dangerous to move until this passes."

Her skin was covered in gooseflesh. If they took off her wet clothes, he had nothing to cover her with. Some Boy Scout he had turned out to be.

Zoe burrowed into his embrace, her teeth chattering audibly. "I don't need a doctor, but I'd kill for a hot shower."

"May I join you?" The words tumbled out. He hadn't meant to say them. But suddenly, despite the wretched conditions, he felt the return of the sexual bond that had taken them both by surprise.

She stroked his collarbone through his shirt. "Why not?" she drawled after a moment. "It's only a fantasy at this point."

"Since you checked into the hotel, I've had lots of fantasies," he confessed. "I believe you must be an Irish fairy in disguise come to grant me three wishes."

He felt her laugh, the sound almost a caress against his chest. "I think one wish is enough. Don't be greedy."

"So will you go with me to New York?"

"I won't be in the way?"

"No."

"Have you ever taken a date to something like this?"

"No."

"Why now? Why me?"

The storm was moving away, the sound of the thunder fading to a muted boom. "I hear the ticking clock," he said, being as honest as he knew how to be. "You won't be in Silver Glen for long. I want a chance to get to know you better."

She sat crossways on his lap, her legs dangling. When his hand brushed her bare thigh, her skin was cold and damp. "I do love New York," she sighed. "I suppose I'll go."

"You don't have to sound so happy about it."

"I'm wet and cold. What do you expect?"

"Now who's the grumpy one?" he asked, grinning though she couldn't see his face.

She pinched his arm. Hard. "You should be nicer to the woman you bumped and made fall down the hill."

"Hey," he said, indignant. "I had nothing to do with it. I can't help it if those new boots tripped you up."

"I'll get more sympathy with the other story."

"Try it and I'll spank you."

"Oooh," she said. "Macho threats. Don't expect me to believe you've read *Fifty Shades of Grey*."

"God, no. I'm more of a John Grisham fan." But should he admit that the idea of turning Zoe's bottom pink turned him on? "We can go now," he said gruffly, desperate to get out of the small, semidark cabin. The only thing keeping his hunger in check at the moment was the lack of a clean flat surface. That and the fact that Zoe might need medical attention.

It wasn't easy for a man to hold a scantily dressed woman in his arms and not think about sex. Particularly if that woman was Zoe Chamberlain. He stood abruptly, lifting her into his arms. "Hang on."

Fortunately for his peace of mind, she was quiet and docile during the trip to the car. The ground was littered with storm debris. Hard-packed dirt had turned rapidly into a mud pit.

After he deposited her in the passenger seat, he ran around to his side, wincing when he realized he had no choice but to put his dirty boots on the mat. If he'd been smart, he'd have brought his Jeep. But he had wanted to pamper Zoe.

He turned on the engine, the heat and the defroster. Zoe had already flipped on her seat warmer. Reaching behind them, he snagged an old sweatshirt. "Here. Put this over your legs. And let me see your hand."

She did as he asked but not without her usual sass. "Bossy, bossy, bossy."

With her small palm turned upward, he examined the series of gouges caused by rocks and whatever else she'd landed on. "I don't think it's going to need stitches, but it's probably going to hurt like hell for a few days. We're lucky you didn't break your arm."

"I'm well aware of that, trust me."

Now that he could see better, he noticed she also had a scrape on the side of her cheek. And there would no doubt be bruises to follow. He glanced down at her leg. "Do you want to try and get that boot off so I can examine your ankle?" How she would do that in the confines of the car, he wasn't sure.

"No, thank you. Let's just get back."

It was a silent drive, each of them lost in thought. A couple of times they ran through rain again. "That ankle needs to be examined." He tried to persuade Zoe to see a doctor, but she flatly refused.

"I'm tired and I want to go to my room. If it's still hurting in the morning, I'll get an X-ray."

"You promise?"

"I do."

When they pulled up at the hotel, Liam handed off the keys to the valet. Zoe insisted on walking up the shallow steps on her own, though she did lean on his arm for support. He escorted her all the way upstairs to the door of her room and halted. "Will you have dinner with me this evening? After you've cleaned up?" He wanted to mention the offer of a shared shower, but he could tell she was drooping.

"I think I'll get room service after a hot soak in the tub. But thank you."

Well, hell. "I understand. Tonight I'll buy a second ticket for New York. The flight is midafternoon. We'll have to leave here at noon in order to drive to the airport in Asheville."

"I'll be ready."

Her body language was screaming at him to back off, but her odd mood disturbed him. What if she chose to bolt? To run away? He brushed the back of his hand down her cheek. "May I come in for a moment?"

Zoe nodded slowly as she inserted her key card. "If you want."

He followed her and shut the door behind him. "I'm sorry our day didn't turn out as planned."

"Life is usually like that," she said.

He looked for irony in her expression, but found none. Zoe had a slant on the world that not many people attained. He wouldn't call it fatalism. That was too negative. What she had was the ability to enjoy the twists and turns, both good and bad, with equanimity. As if everything that happened to her had purpose and value.

Pulling her close, he nuzzled the side of her neck. "I won't keep you. I know you need to get out of those wet clothes."

"I'm fine," she said, but the words were unconvincing.

He kissed her gently, trying to convey feelings that were unformed but strong. She felt good in his arms, as if she had been created to exact specifications that matched needs in his own life he hadn't even known existed.

Holding her like this had a predictable effect on his anatomy. But he wasn't going to push it. Zoe was wet and cold and tired. He forced himself to release her and back step back. "A good day?" He made the words a question.

She nodded. "Of course. I had fun. Despite the weather."

"And the rowdy hikers?"

Her cheeks reddened. In her eyes he saw the memory of almost making love up against a tree. "Their timing could have been better," she agreed, the words wry. Then she shifted gears. "I don't have clothes for New York."

Damn. He should have thought of that. The woman spent part of her nights living in a van, and she had checked into the Silver Beeches with a single suitcase. "Well," he said slowly. "I invited you. So the wardrobe will be my treat. There are several designer boutiques a block from the hotel. We'll go there as soon as we land."

"You won't be buying me clothes. That's ridiculous. I have money. But yes, if I could shop first, that would be helpful."

"Do you?" he said, not pausing to censor the words.

"Do I what?"

"Do you have the money to pay for new clothes?"

He saw her go still, like a wild animal trapped in the headlights of an oncoming car. "I'm staying here, aren't I?"

It wasn't really an answer to his question. "Talk to me, Zoe. If you're strapped for cash, don't rack up a credit card bill for new clothes. It's nothing to be ashamed of."

He was baiting her deliberately. The knowledge made him feel sick, but he was desperate to know the truth. She had given him bits and pieces of her story, but there was more. Something she was withholding. And it involved the cash in the van.

She stared at him, nonplussed. "My finances are in good shape," she said evenly. "But thank you for your concern." The flat words struck him with a force he deserved. Why couldn't he trust her unequivocally?

He was no closer to unraveling the mystery that was Zoe, and yet he had pissed her off. "I'm sorry. I didn't mean to insult you. I only wanted to help."

"You could help by trusting me to manage my own life." The retort was sharp, but he saw humor in her eyes.

"I get the message. Am I forgiven?"

She leaned in and kissed him softly on the cheek. "Of course. Now go before I get hypothermia. I'll talk to you later."

Fourteen

When Zoe awoke the following morning, she practically bounced out of bed. It seemed like days since she had seen Liam, instead of a few hours. He surely had matters to attend to before he could leave town, so she hadn't been surprised not to hear from him.

Her evening had been pleasant enough...and actually cozy. After a hot shower and a change of clothes that finally chased the chills away, she ordered a double serving of mac and cheese along with a big glass of chocolate milk. Wearing her most comfy pajamas as she curled up in the middle of her decadent king-size bed, she had watched half a dozen episodes of her favorite sitcom.

This morning, though, she was ready for adventure. Fortunately, her ankle was almost as good as new. Dressing rapidly in a skirt and top and her favorite gold-and-bronze sandals, she took the time to tidy her belongings and pack everything back into her suitcase. It felt odd leaving this hotel room. In a short amount of time she had made it her own. The only item she would be leaving behind was her precious guitar.

Though she was excited about traveling with Liam, she felt guilty that she was still keeping secrets from him. Last night had been her opportunity to come clean and tell him she was going to leave sooner rather than later. But keeping her own counsel had ensured her safety thus far, and it was a habit hard to break.

Since she skipped breakfast, she went down to the dining room at eleven. Liam hadn't mentioned lunch in their itinerary, and she was starving. As she was enjoying her last cup of coffee, he showed up at her table looking distinctly harried.

"Have you eaten?" she asked.

He didn't sit down. "I'll have to grab something on the plane. It's been a hell of a morning. Somehow we booked an Arabian sheikh and a presidential hopeful in the same suite for the upcoming weekend."

"Oh, good grief."

"I think it happened when we switched over to a new computer system. We've managed to juggle some bookings and comp a few guests for the inconvenience, but the whole fracas ate up my morning."

"Are we still going to make it?"

He leaned down and kissed her cheek. "You can bet on it. Meet me out front in fifteen minutes."

Liam was as good as his word. When Zoe stepped outside, he was standing beside the open door of a limo. She raised an eyebrow. "Is this for us?"

He leaned close and whispered in her ear. "Pierre loves driving it, and it makes him feel good, so who am I to complain?"

Zoe slid into the roomy backseat and sighed. Bessie would be jealous, but Zoe planned to enjoy herself anyway. "Maybe my van will be finished by the time we get back," she said.

"Are you in that much of a hurry?" Liam loosened his tie and reached in the mini fridge for two bottles of water, handing her one.

"I don't like using someone else's car all the time."

"It's a piece of junk."

"Says the man who drives a Jag. The silver Sentra is fine, but I'm not used to accepting favors."

"It's not always a virtue to do everything yourself."

"I'm pretty sure that's a case of the pot calling the kettle black. You don't even trust your mother to run the hotel without you."

His jaw dropped. "That's not true."

"Of course it is. You never travel. You live on the premises. The Silver Beeches Lodge is your baby."

Liam reeled mentally. Could what Zoe accused him of possibly be true? "My mother was grieving when my father died," he said automatically. "It was hard for her to shoulder the responsibility of the hotel without help."

"I'm sure that was true once upon a time. But she's still a young woman. And from what I can tell, she's smart and energetic and capable. Maybe she doesn't want to hurt your feelings by telling you she can carry on without you."

He leaned back in his corner and toyed with the cap of his water bottle. It was okay for him to psychoanalyze Zoe, but when she turned the tables, he didn't much like it.

Perhaps sensing his mood, Zoe ignored him, doing something on her phone. The uneasy silence lasted all the way to Asheville, through security at the airport and onto the jet. Liam took the window seat in first class, leaving Zoe to chat cheerfully with the male flight attendant. The man was under her spell in five minutes.

Disgruntled and inexplicably irritable, Liam closed his eyes and pretended to sleep.

* * *

Zoe loved to fly. The sensation of speed at takeoff, the beauty of sailing above the clouds, the anticipation of an exciting destination at journey's end…all of it gave her a buzz unlike most anything else.

It was disappointing that Liam had chosen to sleep. She had hoped to chat with him about what they might do when his meeting was over. But she had to be content with reading the in-flight magazine cover to cover and sipping a Diet Coke.

The trip north was smooth, despite a hurried connection in Atlanta. The landing at LaGuardia was textbook. Neither she nor Liam had any carry-on bags other than Zoe's purse. After they retrieved their luggage, they met a private car near the taxi stand. Liam gave an address on the Upper East Side. In moments they were speeding toward the city.

And still Liam hadn't said a word. Finally, his silence began to make her mad. "You don't have to sulk merely because I pointed out the obvious."

He glared at her. "I am *not* sulking. I have a lot on my mind."

"Whatever." She turned her attention out the window, noting the frantic traffic and congested roadways that were so unlike western North Carolina. Perhaps she should try living in New York for a while. There were thousands of venues here for aspiring musicians who were willing to play for little or nothing. Maybe a change of scenery would do her good.

She was taken totally off guard when a big hand grasped her wrist and tugged. "Come closer," Liam said.

Now almost in his lap, she glared. "What are you doing?"

His smile was lopsided. "Apologizing. And kissing you."

"But I—"

Two fingers touched her lips. "Shhh," he crooned. "Let me grovel."

When his mouth settled over hers, she could have sworn that the chauffeur began driving erratically. Her stomach flipped in dizzying loops and her heart raced. The setting was not exactly private. Liam didn't seem to mind. He was barely touching her, but she began to melt.

That a man could convey so much in a kiss was eye opening. He kissed her sweetly but desperately, as if trying to convince himself or her that what they had was going to last. She clung to his waist, attempting to maintain some semblance of dignity. "I think the driver is watching us in the mirror," she whispered.

"No, he's not." Liam's sharp teeth nipped her lower lip. "Close your eyes, Zoe."

She obeyed his command, not because she wanted to, but because she had no choice. His taste seduced her, as did his touch. And the sound of his harsh breathing told her she wasn't alone in the midst of this sensual exploration. The wine-dark river of pleasure that Liam conjured made her move restlessly, her knees bumping his.

"Are we almost there?" she asked, wanting to unbutton his shirt and stroke his warm, hard chest. His suave facade seemed nothing more than a thin veneer at the moment. In every way he was a male predator, and he had fixed his sights on her.

Liam nodded, his teeth raking a sensitive spot on her neck. Pulling away suddenly, he sighed, his chest heaving. "You'd better do something to your hair."

She took a mirrored compact from her purse and felt her face go hot when she saw her reflection. Her lips were swollen, her eyes hazy. While she managed some quick repair work, Liam gently smoothed her skirt where he had shifted it to caress her bare thighs. His hands were warm against her skin.

Moments later, the car pulled up in front of a small, elegant hotel tucked beneath the shadow of two larger buildings. Colorful flags hung from a parapet over the main entrance. Enormous planters shaped like lions flanked the

glass doorway, only partially constraining masses of bego-
nias, tulips and hyacinths.

Liam took care of the fare and gave Zoe a hand as she
climbed out. A smiling doorman welcomed them while a
bellman hurried forward to take their luggage.

At the front desk, Liam handed over a platinum card. His
hold on Zoe's hand was firm enough to make her wince.
When the clerk apologized profusely because their room
would not be ready for an hour, Zoe had to bite her lip to
keep from laughing at the look on Liam's face.

She patted his arm. "It's okay. We'll shop first."

There was a certain look a man got when he was fixated
on carnal matters. Liam had it. "Fine," he grumbled, not
quite managing a smile for the poor hotel employee.

Outside on the sidewalk, Zoe dared to tease him. "We'll
have all night for what you have in mind."

Liam's expression went from thundercloud to mildly irritated. "Is that a promise?"

She rested her cheek on his shoulder for a brief moment.
"I think that it is."

Liam relaxed in an armchair and sipped the champagne
supplied by an obsequious woman whose eyeglasses were
an unlikely shade of neon-green. If that was the big color
on the runway this year, he had to hope Zoe wasn't a slave
to fashion.

His little flower child wandered around the shop, her lips
pursed, as she examined one thing after another. This was
the third boutique they had visited. The first one had been
big on rivets and studs. Zoe had turned up her nose. The
next one had had a definite Jackie Kennedy vibe, which as
Zoe pointed out, was beautiful, but not her style.

This particular establishment seemed more her speed.
"So what do I need?" she asked, her attention focused on a
rack of gowns.

"Two nice dresses for daywear, and two fancy ones for

the evenings." He was looking forward to showing her off. Zoe's fresh charm would be a hit among his colleagues. The group was mixed, about half female and half male. That all of them would be enchanted by his date, he had no doubt.

With the saleslady's help, Zoe collected an armful of clothing and headed for the fitting rooms. "I'm going to start with these."

"Make sure you come show them to me," he said. If he were being forced to shop instead of make love to Zoe, he might as well get something out of the experience.

She started with the regular outfits, the first one a traditional *little black dress* that fit her beautifully. The hem stopped just above the knees. "What do you think?" she asked.

He cocked his head and studied her. The more sophisticated attire made her seem older, but didn't detract from her appeal. "Perfect for the meeting."

Next was a more casual striped frock in yellow and cinnamon and orange that hearkened back to the days of Grace Kelly. Spaghetti straps held up a fitted bodice that flared out in a short, flirty skirt underlain with multicolored petticoats. Forget Grace Kelly. Zoe's smile made him think of Audrey Hepburn, all innocent delight.

Though she went through several more choices, they both decided that the first two were the best. For a moment, he debated asking her if she wanted to try on lingerie, but doubtless that would embarrass her. When Zoe switched to evening gowns, Liam knew he was in trouble. She looked amazing in everything she put on.

Even so, some were easily discarded. The ones with too many beads and sequins tended to overpower her delicate frame. Gradually she gravitated toward choices that were exceedingly plain on the hanger, but transformed when Zoe modeled them.

She came out in a fire-engine-red number that dried his throat. The collar fastened high on her neck, but the arms and shoulders had been cut away, barely leaving enough fabric to mold to her firm breasts and to cover her shoulder blades. The skirt was fluid and slit to midthigh. "How about this one?" she asked.

"Do *you* like it?"

Glancing in the three-way mirror, she looked over her shoulder and studied the image of her backside. "This is definitely a grown-up dress."

He smiled at the doubt in her voice. "I have every confidence you can pull it off, sweet Zoe. Now pick one more and we'll be done."

The clerk, already sniffing a fat commission, refilled his glass. "Your young lady is lovely, Mr. Kavanagh."

"Yes, she is," he said softly.

In moments, Zoe changed and tiptoed out one last time, stopping to look at her reflection. Their eyes met in the mirror, his hot and hungry, hers filled with a dawning awareness of the sexual power she wielded.

The final gown was a brilliant aquamarine that complemented her blond hair beautifully. It was made almost like a wedding dress, strapless, cinched at the waist, and with a skirt that billowed in layers of tulle on top of silk and taffeta.

Zoe twirled, an involuntary motion that brought a smile to his face. He wondered if he handed the saleswoman a wad of bills if she would agree to close the store and disappear for an hour. Liam was imagining everything he could do *to* and *with* Zoe in view of those three mirrors.

He cleared his throat. "I don't think there's any question," he said gruffly. "That dress was meant for you."

Zoe's starry-eyed gaze tangled with his. She wet her lips. "I feel like a princess." Smoothing the skirt with both hands, she lifted her shoulders and let them fall. "This dress costs more than my van."

"I told you it was my treat."

She shook her head vehemently. "No. If I'm going to live outrageously, it will be on my dime." She turned the saleslady. "All four of these, please. I'll be out in a moment to pay."

The older woman hurried to zip the couture gowns and dresses into clear garment bags. Zoe handed out the last one and appeared moments later, back in her own clothes.

"I'd forgotten how lovely it is to dress up. Makes a woman feel special."

He stood and put his hands on her shoulders, moving behind her as they faced the mirror. "You *are* special," he murmured. "Very special."

Nothing about their current situation was conducive to intimacy, but he was not going to be able to wait much longer. Zoe made him hunger in a way he couldn't quite fathom. Sexual desire was a common thing for a man, an ingrained component of the Y chromosome. Men could look at a stranger crossing the street, a girl in a magazine ad, an actress in a movie…and get aroused. It was predictable and inevitable.

But with Zoe, something else happened. Something he didn't quite understand. All he knew was that she made him tremble with lust. How could he be rigid with passion and yet incredibly weak at the same time? In her presence he experienced the full measure of his masculinity and a simultaneous and inescapably humbling recognition of his vulnerability where she was concerned.

Before he could do something foolish like drag Zoe back into one of those little dressing rooms with the fancy gold doors, the store employee returned, taking Zoe's card and running it through a nearby register. "Would you like me to have these delivered?" she asked, finishing the transaction and producing Zoe's receipt.

Liam nodded. "In the morning will be fine." He gave the hotel's address, and finally, they were back out on the street. He looked down at Zoe. "Would you like to have dinner somewhere nice? See a play? My evenings are all yours, even if I do have to pay attention to business during the day."

All around them, crowds of people passed by. Not the manic movement of Times Square. Just a steady stream of men and women returning home from a busy day. He and Zoe created an island of calm. She took one of his hands and lifted it to her lips. "At the risk of sounding incredibly gauche and boring, I was thinking we might order room service and then have an early night."

Fifteen

Zoe knew she had made the right choice when Liam's eyes darkened to navy and his strong cheekbones went ruddy with color. "I brought you here to have a good time," he said, clearly trying to be a gentleman.

She went up on tiptoe and pressed a kiss to his firm, wonderful lips. "I've been to New York City before. And there are a lot of ways to have a good time."

Liam held her at arms' length, staring at her intently as if he could read some secret in her eyes. "You amaze me. Everything is more fun with you. How do you do that?"

"I don't know. But I think it's both of us together. When I first met you, I thought we were too different, but maybe that's what makes it work."

"C'mon," he said, slinging an arm around her shoulders. "If our room is not ready now, we're going somewhere else."

Zoe decided to let Liam take the lead in what happened next. Not that she thought a woman couldn't initiate sex. But he seemed to be on a short fuse, and it might be fun to be wooed. Fortunately for her companion's peace of mind, one of the two penthouse suites awaited them. Their French doors opened out onto a lovely rooftop garden. Though the view was blocked by other structures, the spot was intimate and appealing.

After Liam gave a terse nod of approval to the terrace, he tipped the bellman generously and ushered him out the door. Zoe watched from a distance as her would-be lover investigated the spacious accommodations. His one glimpse into the sybaritic bedroom was short. She gauged his mood pretty well. Perhaps room service could come afterward.

Stepping back inside and locking the double glass doors, she leaned against them. Her earlier burst of confidence had winnowed away. Liam's brooding intensity churned all sorts of feelings in her belly. She wanted him desperately, and yet some primitive female reaction to the male's arousal abashed her and kept her from making a move.

He ripped off his tie and tossed it on an antique escritoire. Next followed his conservative jacket. It landed short of an ottoman. Liam made no move to retrieve it. His manner was agitated. "What do you want to order for dinner?" he asked gruffly, not looking at her.

"Um…"

The air in the room was charged with something fierce, something erotic. She didn't know how to respond. Or perhaps she knew but was afraid. And with every second that passed, Liam shed another layer of civility. He prowled like a fierce animal.

Whirling to face her suddenly, he lifted a dark eyebrow. "What did you say?"

"Well, I…"

"You pick," he said impatiently. "I don't care what we eat. I'm going to take a shower while you order."

Before she could say a word, he disappeared.

The air whooshed from her lungs audibly. She hadn't even realized she was holding her breath. Never had she felt less like eating dinner. So that was that. She refused to pick up the phone. Because she was fairly certain that Liam had no interest in food either.

But without a meal to ease the way with social convention, what was her next move? Stealthily, she hung out a do-not-disturb sign and locked the door firmly, bolting it for good measure. She did use the phone after all, but only to call the front desk and ask not to be disturbed. With the sun still shining brightly, though low in the sky, the request seemed extremely wicked and daring.

Any moment now, Liam would reappear, so she had to decide her course. Gazing at her reflection in the large ornate mirror that hung over the sofa in the outer salon, she began to take off her clothes.

Liam remained beneath the icy cold spray for longer than necessary, trying to tame the raging beast of lust and desire that made him tremble. He wanted Zoe so badly, he feared overwhelming her.

Taking his sex in his hands, he thought about relieving some of his agitation in the shower. His erection was full and heavy, the skin taut and sensitive. But when he moved his fingers restlessly up the shaft, he realized that he wanted Zoe's hands on his body more than he wanted momentary release.

Shivering beneath the frigid water, he soaped himself and washed his hair. By rights, this punishment should have helped. But when he got out and dried off, his need was not diminished in any way.

The hotel had provided plush robes in male and female sizes. He put on the larger of the two and scraped his hands through his hair. Planning to dress quickly and meet Zoe back out in the salon, he opened the bathroom door and padded barefoot into the bedroom.

Stopping dead in his tracks, he felt his mouth go dry and his throat tighten. "Zoe," he said hoarsely.

"I was hoping for more of a reaction than that," she said, her smile cheeky. But in her eyes he saw the same vulnerability that had attracted him in the beginning and made him want to protect her at all costs.

Her pose was designed to seduce. Propped up in a nest of pillows against the headboard, her naked beauty caught him off guard. He rested one hand against the armoire, more for support than anything else. Her bare breasts were as perfect as any classical statue, but warm and pink, the visage mouth-watering.

Leaving his robe on for the moment was a tactical choice. He moved toward the bed, wondering if he could keep her here for a week, a month, forever. "I thought you wanted dinner," he said, realizing as he uttered the words that they were ridiculous and unnecessary. Zoe had made her wishes more than clear.

She patted the mattress beside her. "All I want is you, Liam Kavanagh. Come woo me with that famous Irish charm."

"I'm feeling more like a Viking marauder." The flat statement was entirely true. And should have warned her that she was in danger. But his reference to their fantasy play the first time they made love made her laugh softly.

"Then perhaps you should tie me up. So I don't try to murder you with a poison dagger." She held out her hand, and he saw for the first time that she had a couple of ties, obviously filched from his suitcase. They were silk. Ridiculously expensive.

"Why didn't I think of that?" The words came out hoarse and ragged. Breathing was difficult. Resting one knee on the bed, he took the ties and examined his options. The headboard was solid, but each corner was adorned with an ornamental spindle. If the mattress had been a king, this little game wouldn't have worked.

Their suite, however, was decorated in antiques, and the

ornate bed was a queen. Which meant that if he spread Zoe's arms wide, he could restrain her easily enough.

Fastening the strips of cloth around her wrists and securing them to the wooden anchors gave him an entirely Neanderthal rush of exhilaration. She looked up at him the entire time, her sky-blue irises almost obscured by the dilation of her dark pupils. The only sign that she might be at all alarmed was the way her small white teeth worried her lower lip.

Sitting back on his haunches when the deed was done, he stared at her. It was like giving a starving man access to a smorgasbord. He didn't know where to start first.

Zoe was silent, her chest rising and falling rapidly. "Are you cold?" she asked politely.

He lifted an eyebrow. "Not even a little." In fact, he felt like he was burning up from the inside out.

"Then why don't you ditch that robe?"

Without leaving the bed, he shrugged out of the heavy terry garment and tossed it aside. Zoe's eyes widened a fraction more as her gaze landed on his erection. It grew beneath her appreciative regard. Her legs moved restlessly against the soft sheets.

The air was redolent with the scent of desire and the fragrance of lilacs in the arrangement of fresh flowers tucked in a crystal vase across the room. Nature's perfume would mark his sensory memory forever.

He was not sure how long he hovered on the edge of reason. The room was silent but for the tick of a mantel clock. Outside, traffic rushed madly, but the cacophony of blaring horns and squealing brakes was muted and distant, barely impinging on his consciousness.

He ran a hand down her hip to her thigh to her ankle. "Are you comfortable?" he asked, not quite able to make the full leap to realistic barbarian.

"Does it matter?"

The taunt snapped what little control he had left. "I suppose not." Sliding down in the bed, he positioned his body between her legs and maneuvered until he could taste her intimately. With the first pass of his tongue, she cried out.

He stopped and lifted his head. "Perhaps I should have gagged you," he said, injecting silky menace into the words.

Her whole body quivered. "No. Please. I'll be quiet."

The begging added a nice touch. Without responding, he returned to his enjoyable task, trying to make her lose her senses. Her sex was moist and swollen, clear evidence of her arousal. The taste went to his head like strong liquor. When he bit gently at the one spot that begged for his attention, Zoe's back arched as she groaned and thrust helplessly against his mouth while he coaxed the last ounce of response from her quivering body.

In the aftermath, he rested his head on her hot, damp thigh, listening to the beat of his own heart. The frantic thuds raged like the waterfalls that crashed down the mountains as the snow melted. No longer able to defer his own need for release, he moved away only a moment to don a condom. Then he came down on top of her, supporting most of his weight on his elbows. Her body was a welcoming foil to his.

They were nose to nose. So close he could see the blond tips of her darker eyelashes.

Zoe moistened her lips with her tongue. "If you need a reference next time you go out marauding, I'll be happy to testify on your behalf." Her words were husky and low.

He pressed his mouth to hers softly. Tenderness mingled with impatient arousal, tempering his urgency. "I may retire," he said. "I've heard the life span of a Viking is pretty short and I don't want to miss a minute of this." Raining butterfly kisses across her nose, her cheeks, her forehead, he tried to convey what he couldn't put into words.

But soon, the feel of her soft belly pressing against his erection derailed his efforts to be gentle. With one hand, he opened her passage and pressed inward.

Zoe gasped.

Everything about the first time they made love faded away, and he moved in her as if this was brand-new. An unminted experience. A story waiting to be told. The pleasure was intense, each moment layering upon the next with hushed anticipation.

The muscles in Zoe's arms quivered visibly as she pulled at her restraints. The evidence of her wild impatience shored up his desire to make the intimacy last. "I can do anything I want to you," he said, pausing to wet one pert nipple with a swirl of his tongue. "You're completely helpless. Totally at my mercy. Every inch of you belongs to me."

"Barbarian," she hissed. But it was a weak protest at best. The rosy tint to her cheeks told him she was enjoying the pretense.

"All men are barbarians beneath the skin," he said. You can dress us up and tame us like lap dogs, but at the first opportunity, we'll grab for what we want." He withdrew almost completely and slid back in to torment them both. "And I want you." The squeeze of her inner passage around his rigid flesh was intense. He wanted to come more than he wanted his next breath, but he couldn't bear to end it. Not yet.

"Untie me," she pleaded. "I want to touch you."

"You should have thought of that when you devised this little game." Leaning to one side, he ran one of his hands from her shoulder up her arm to her wrist. Twining her fingers with his, he thrust lazily. "I'll make you come again," he promised.

Her eyelids fluttered shut on a sigh. "I can't." The pout of her lips was petulant.

"Why not?" If the involuntary clasp of her body on his was any indication, she was well on her way.

"I won't let myself receive pleasure from a barbarian."

He chuckled, returning to his earlier position and picking up the pace. "Wanna bet?"

Humor fled in the face of dark, urgent hunger. His control snapped, and he slammed into her repeatedly. Heat rose in his belly, spread to his loins and sent flash fire to his sex. Dimly he realized that Zoe's inner muscles gripped him tightly as she climaxed, but he was lost in a physical bliss so pure it seemed impossible.

When he finally regained his senses, remorse swamped him. Her arms must be aching like hell. "I need to untie you," he muttered, his words slurred with exhaustion. He felt boneless, as if she had sapped every bit of stamina he possessed.

When he thought he could stand, he rose to his feet and disposed of the condom. As he came back to deal with his prisoner, he saw that his neckwear had been rendered unusable for anything other than erotic fun and games.

Because of the way Zoe had writhed and struggled, the knots were tight. He picked at them impatiently, already wanting her again.

She pursed her lips, a frown marking a tiny crease between her brows. "Shouldn't you have a knife to cut me free?"

"I'm pretty sure TSA wouldn't have approved that in my carry-on. Be still, will you? I'm never going to get these loose at this rate."

Zoe stared at him wide-eyed. "Are you in a hurry?"

Her innocence was not convincing. "Yes, damn it. I'd advise not testing my patience."

"Duly noted." The snappy response was designed to irritate him. And it worked.

When he finally got the first knot undone and unwrapped the tie from Zoe's arm, he was chagrined to see the deep red marks on her wrist. Were barbarians capable of feeling remorse? Probably not.

He smoothed his thumb over the damage. "Is it sore?" Even knowing he had given her two satisfying orgasms, the visible result of their love play distressed him.

Twisting her wrist to get the blood flowing, Zoe curled a hand behind his neck and pulled him down for a kiss. He went willingly, ignoring the fact that he still had one knot to go.

"It's fine," she said. "I'm fine." At that very moment, her stomach rumbled loudly.

Obviously, he needed to feed his captive. There were rules about that kind of thing. Liam reluctantly released her and struggled with her other hand, this one taking him even longer. "If we do this again," he grumbled, "we're going to use professional equipment."

Zoe raised an eyebrow. "Someone makes professional *barbarian* equipment?"

"I haven't actually seen such a thing, but I'm betting that on the internet you can find just about anything."

At last, he freed her. Zoe crossed her arms across her chest. As if he hadn't seen everything there was to see already. For a split second he debated initiating an immediate round three. But then he thought better of it. If they were going to keep this up all night, they needed calories.

He climbed out of bed despite the fact that every instinct told him to stay. "I'll leave the bathroom to you for now. Do you trust me to order dinner for us?"

She nodded, now with the sheet pulled all the way to her shoulders. "I'll eat pretty much anything except for lima beans and tofu. But make sure there's lots of whatever you order. And chocolate. And wine."

Bending to pick up the robe he had tossed on the floor, he shrugged into it, belting the waist. "Anything else?"

"Some strawberries wouldn't hurt. And maybe some whipped cream. You never know when that might come in handy."

He stared at her. "Are we talking about dinner or sex?"

"Dinner first. Then more sex. But we might save the fruit for later."

Hands on his hips, he regarded her, shaking his head. "I don't know where I ever got the idea you were a sweet, innocent woman. But I like the way you think. How do you feel about bananas?"

"I put a condom on one once in health class."

"Was it good for you?"

She burst out laughing. "I don't know where I ever got the idea you were a serious-minded stuffed shirt."

"Turns out, we were both wrong."

Although they weren't touching, he experienced the oddest feeling of connection. For this one moment, they were in perfect accord. His ancestors would have called it fate. Or a gift from the fairies. Liam preferred to think of it as destiny. Fate was a whimsical, occasionally coldhearted bitch. But a man could control his own destiny.

"There's a robe for you in the bathroom," he said. "But don't get too attached to it. My plans for later include you being naked."

Sixteen

Zoe freshened up and donned the soft, comfy robe, flipping her hair over the collar. One look in the mirror told her she looked exactly like what she was…a woman who had spent several hours in bed with her lover.

She was sore in more places than her wrists, but it was a good kind of sore…the sort of feeling that curved her mouth in a smug smile.

After splashing her face with water and brushing her hair, she spritzed her wrists with perfume and used a bit of gloss on her puffy lips. Now, her reflection was more like the usual Zoe.

When she entered the living room area of their suite, Liam was clearing a spot by the window for their meal. He looked over his shoulder as she entered. "Should be here soon."

She perched on the arm of the sofa, enjoying the view. Liam in that robe was only slightly less yummy than naked Liam. But before she could go too far with that particular fantasy, a knock sounded at the door.

The young man who rolled a serving cart into their room and uncovered the dishes never batted an eye at their dishabille. Presumably he was used to the eccentricities of hotel guests. But Zoe couldn't help feeling a bit embarrassed. With the do-not-disturb sign on the door and the robes she and Liam were wearing, the guy had to know they'd been having sex.

Even a more seasoned employee would have goggled at the tip Liam handed over. The kid's effusive thanks were still bubbling when Liam eased him out the door and shut it behind him.

"How much *was* that?" Zoe asked.

Liam shrugged, his grin wide. "A couple hundred. I'm in a good mood. Come sit down before everything gets cold."

The meal was a hodgepodge of delights. Thinly shaved prime rib on homemade rolls, fresh asparagus and cinnamon apples were Zoe's favorites. "You've been paying attention to what I order at the Silver Beeches," she accused, suddenly realizing that such appealing choices couldn't have been entirely random.

Liam nodded, entirely unrepentant. "Of course. It's my job to make you happy."

"I like the sound of that."

With tousled hair and the shadow of a late-day beard darkening his chin, Liam was the epitome of a lazy, satisfied predator. A lion maybe, relaxing in his domain before his next hunting mission. He ate with gusto, devouring twice as much as she did, and draining a bottle of wine with a little help from her.

Over dessert, chocolate cake filled with dark-chocolate ganache, they chatted lazily of this and that. Silver Glen. Dylan's bar. Politics. The books they had read and liked.

When she was feeling completely mellow and utterly content with life, Liam dropped an unexpected bomb. "May I ask you a personal question?" he said.

She stiffened automatically. Though she knew intellectually that he had no wish to harm her, her shields went up. "I suppose."

"You're an only child…right?"

"Yes."

"So when your father dies, his company will go to you and your mother…or only you if she is gone."

"Yes. What's your point?" She was not happy that he had decided to introduce this topic in the midst of their romantic idyll.

Liam sipped his coffee, his eyes meeting hers over the rim of his cup. "Has it ever occurred to you that if you cooperate with him now, you might be able to shape the company and help steer it in the direction you want it to go?"

A knot of hurt formed in her stomach. Clearly Liam hadn't understood the full measure of her father's ruthless determination. "I don't want the company," she said flatly. "And no. I have no wish to cooperate with him. I tried plenty of times when I was younger, believe me."

"I know it's hard, but he's your family, no matter how much you dislike his methods. Are you sure you want to permanently sever that tie?"

Her fists were clenched in her lap where he couldn't see. And though his perspective was understandable, she wished that just once in her life someone would take her side.

"You don't understand," she said quietly. "You come from a family where support is freely given, where you all love each other despite your differences. My father is not like that. My mother and I are little more than chattels to him, incidental pawns in his game."

"That's a pretty cynical view."

"And you're being presumptuous. You know nothing at all about my life. So I'd appreciate it if you would resist the urge to pass judgment."

"For God's sake, I'm not judging you."

"You *are*," she cried passionately. "Your father was a disappointment to you, but instead of writing off the Kavanagh empire, you sacrificed your dreams on the altar of filial responsibility. That was *your* choice. But it's not mine. I've seen the world and had some amazing experiences. I haven't allowed my father to dictate who I am or what I make of my life. I've been free."

"You call roving from town to town, always looking over your shoulder being free?"

Zoe's face went white, and Liam knew he had gone too far. Her family situation was not his business. He understood that. But she wore loneliness like a hair shirt, and it hurt him to see her that way. "I'm sorry," he said.

She stood up, her eyes bleak. "Me, too. I'm going to pack and catch a late flight back. You can call and cancel the dress order."

"Now wait a damn minute."

Though she had been halfway to the bedroom, she stopped. "There's nothing more to say."

"So we disagree about something and our relationship is over? Is that it?"

"There's no relationship, Liam. You're in charge of your realm and I'm passing through. It was never going to be anything else."

He approached her slowly, knowing it was going to take a miracle to make her to stay. "Then give me this interlude to remember you by...two more days. I swear I won't say another word about your father."

"Why? What's the point?"

"Because I won't let you go. Not now. Not tonight." Scooping her up in his arms, he carried her to their bedroom. Something eased inside him when he felt her arms loop around his neck. "I can make you happy, Zoe. I promise."

For the next forty-eight hours he did exactly that. With a mutual unspoken agreement between them not to delve into sensitive topics, they set out to enjoy one of the greatest cities in the world.

First on the agenda the following day was his luncheon keynote. Zoe sat in the audience looking prim and perfect in her new black dress while Liam struggled to keep his mind on what he had to say. People seemed to like the speech. There were cordial handshakes and a few hugs, and plenty of hearty congratulations. At least half of the group lingered to be introduced to a blushing Zoe.

She was charming and funny and perfectly at home in this world of movers and shakers. After everything she had told him, he knew his initial assessment of her background had been comically off the mark. Zoe might have spent some time living in her van, but it wasn't because she came from impoverished beginnings.

During the afternoon they returned to the hotel for another round of sweaty, wonderful sex followed by a shower and a nap. He lay with her in his arms, trying to wrap his head around the sea change in his life. In a dramatically short time, Zoe had shattered the notion that his life was complete.

She had danced into his world like the brightest of butterflies, the most brilliant of flowers, showing him by sheer virtue of contrast what he had been missing. His brain whirled with possibilities, but he knew in his heart that until Zoe settled things with her father, either a reconciliation or a total break, she would never be able to settle down.

And what about her mother? The questions went on and on.

The following day was much like the day before, except that instead of the luncheon, he dropped Zoe at the Met while he pursued a very important errand. Once he returned, he spent another hour with Zoe wandering the museum before they finally went in search of food.

The day was sunny and bright, so they bought hot dogs from a vendor in the Central Park and watched dads and kids sail model boats on the lake. Zoe's face was wistful. "They look so happy."

He wanted to ask what her childhood had been like, but he had promised not to talk about her father anymore. It was hard to imagine any parent not being delighted with the child Zoe must have been.

"Come on," he said, linking his hand with hers. "You look sleepy." They had been out late the night before, taking in a Broadway show and dinner afterward.

They caught a cab and were back at their hotel in no time. As soon as the door to their suite closed, Zoe threw herself into his arms. "I want to make love to you," she said, her expression cajoling.

Didn't she know that no persuasion was necessary? Intimacy with Zoe was never far from his mind.

Allowing her to take him by the hand and lead him to the bedroom, he hid a smile when she began unbuttoning his shirt with sweet concentration. The touch of her hands made him inhale sharply. Would it always be like this? She had woven some kind of magic, invisible chains around him, and he was a willing victim.

When they were both naked, he lifted her in his arms and carried her to the bed. "You are the most beautiful thing I've ever seen," he said, resting his forehead on hers.

As he bent to deposit her on the mattress, she scooted over to make room for him. They came together in mutual accord, silently, slowly, the moment filled with yearning and poignancy. Somehow he had to get through to her. But that could wait.

Her slim legs tightened around his waist as he canted her hips, deepening the penetration. Her golden hair fanned out across the pillow. This room had become their haven, their escape from the realities of a world that was not always kind to hopes and dreams.

The end this time was more of a gently rolling wave, sweeping them onto a distant shore of contentment. Zoe curled into his embrace. They dozed for half an hour. Liam slipped in and out of sleep. He didn't want to miss a moment of what might be his last time with her.

When she roused, he brushed the hair from her face. "I want to ask you something."

Yawning, she ran her toes down his shin. "Okay."

"I want you to stay at the hotel for longer than six weeks. My treat. Better yet, in my apartment. And if you like, we can move your mother to Silver Beeches as well. Perhaps a change of scenery could help her see that she needs to leave your father."

Zoe played with the hair on his chest. "I don't know if she would come."

"And you?"

The silence was long. Scary. But finally, she nodded. "I could do that."

"Good. I'm glad." He left it at that. He was afraid if he made too big a deal of her consent it would spook her.

By the time they returned to Silver Glen, he and Zoe were comfortable with each other in a way he wouldn't have been able to manage with her as a guest in his hotel. They had created a special kind of intimacy in New York. When she wore the blue dress the final night, he had taken her to a gala fund-raiser for a charitable foundation. They had danced until 2:00 a.m. and had gone back to their hotel to sleep and make love and sleep again.

Now, on the plane back to North Carolina, he began to feel a sense of dread. He couldn't quite say why. Zoe sat in the seat beside him sleeping peacefully, her head resting on his shoulder. Nothing had changed. Perhaps it was a taste of regret for having to leave the city where they had forged a tenuous accord. That and the realization that he still had unanswered questions about Zoe's father and how she intended to handle him.

Because their flight had been delayed indefinitely in

Charlotte, Liam had called Pierre and told him not to bother meeting them. After they deplaned and claimed their luggage, Liam rented a car and soon they were on their way home.

Zoe was awake now, but quiet, her gaze trained out the window, though it was dark. It irked him that he never knew what she was thinking. Just when he began to think he knew her well, she threw him off balance in one way or another.

Back at the Silver Beeches, the facade of the hotel was lit up. Liam felt the sensation of homecoming and yet had no real urge to stop by the front desk and check on things as would have been his usual habit. All he could think about was taking Zoe upstairs to bed. His or hers. It didn't matter.

While he was passing off his keys to the valet, Pierre came rushing out of the hotel. The dignified man never hurried anywhere, so Liam's radar went up. The concierge lowered his voice as he came closer. "A man who appears to be Ms. Chamberlain's father is here. He's in the lobby refusing to leave until he sees her. And he's threatening to call the police and accuse you of kidnapping."

"What a load of crap." Liam debated rapidly. "We'll go in the side door and head to my office. That will give Zoe a few minutes to collect her thoughts. Is that okay with you, Zoe?"

She was standing on the opposite side of the car, her hand resting on the hood. "Oh, so I get a vote?"

The acerbic words reminded him that she didn't like to be coddled. "Sorry. What do *you* want to do?"

"I don't want to see my father, but I knew this showdown was coming sooner or later. It's probably for the best, anyway. I'm not going to be afraid of him anymore. I'm an adult woman. It's time he knows that he can't use me as a pawn in his games."

Liam looked at Pierre. "Stall him a little longer. Tell him Zoe just got in and she's freshening up."

"Yes, sir."

Pierre disappeared as Liam took Zoe by the arm and led

her into the relative safety of the shadowy side courtyard. Before they went inside, he stopped short, having just had an epiphany that shocked him. "Zoe," he said urgently. "Is it true that you've been living off the grid for the last eighteen months?"

He felt her nod. "More or less. Why?"

"When you came to Silver Beeches, you used a credit card…a traceable credit card."

"I'm sure you wouldn't have let me check in without it."

"That's not my point. Were you somehow subconsciously setting up a confrontation with your father? You had to know that if he hired someone to trace your whereabouts from place to place that he would have no compunction about investigating you in other ways."

"So?"

"So I'm asking if my theory is true."

"If it is, I didn't do it deliberately. Can we please go inside now? I'm getting chilly."

Zoe felt as if she were walking in a nightmare. But there would be no waking up from this. The last thing she wanted was for Liam and her father to meet. It embarrassed her that the Kavanaghs were such a wonderful family, and her own father was a bully and a mean-spirited dictator.

In Liam's office she sat in a chair, her knees wobbly and her hands icy cold. Dealing with her father was never pleasant, but coming on the heels of the wonderful hours spent with Liam in New York, this encounter was going to be particularly bleak.

Liam knelt in front of her, his eyes watchful, but kind. "How can I help?"

She shrugged, not quite able to meet his gaze. "I don't know. I guess it depends on whether he still plans to arrest me."

Liam flinched. She saw it and felt it.

"Look at me, Zoe." He stood and pulled her to her feet.

"Before anything else happens, I want you to know that I love you."

Shock rendered her boneless. Her legs threatened to collapse beneath her. "Your timing sucks," she said, staring at him, her voice hoarse with tears. Of all the times she had daydreamed about hearing him say those words, the scenario had never been this. "Why are you telling me now?"

His smile was lopsided. "Well, for one, it's true. But before you go in to see your father, I want you to know that whatever happens, I'll be there for you."

She shook her head, confused and anxious. "I don't understand. What do you think is going to happen?"

Easing her back into the chair, he pulled another chair up beside her so he could hold her hands, warming them between his. "I know about the money, Zoe."

She stared at him blankly. "What money?"

Now he looked grim. "You said your father accused you of taking money from him."

"But I didn't." He wasn't making sense.

"Zoe." He stopped, looked down at their hands, and shook his head slowly. "It's okay, sweetheart. You aren't in this alone. You don't have to pretend with me. I love you."

Truly bewildered, she searched his face. "I don't have a clue what you're talking about."

For the first time, he let his frustration and disappointment show through his mask of caring. "I *know* about the money, Zoe. I know you have it. Gary found it when he was getting ready to paint the van."

"And he told you?"

"Yes. He was worried about it. But it's okay. We'll tell your father you didn't spend it. That you took it because you were angry. We'll give it back. And if necessary, I'll hire you the best lawyer we can find. I won't let your father hurt you."

Zoe stared at him aghast, all her dreams disintegrating around her like hundreds of falling stars. "You think I stole from my father. Even though I told you I didn't."

His jaw was granite, his eyes pools of something…regret, maybe. "People do crazy things when they get pushed into a corner. I don't blame you. Really."

"How generous of you." She stood up, no longer aware of any emotion at all. She was encased in ice. "I will see my father now."

"Wait," Liam said, lurching to his feet and grabbing her by the shoulders. "I told you I love you. Doesn't that warrant a response of some sort?"

She smiled at him politely, as she would a stranger. "Of course, it does…. Go to hell, Liam."

Seventeen

He chased her down the hallway to the lobby, his emotions reeling. What in the devil was going on?

Before he could stop her, Zoe walked right up to a distinguished gray-haired man and greeted him evenly. "Hello, Father. I hear you've been looking for me."

The elder Henshaw seemed taken aback. Zoe was wearing one of the dresses she had picked out in New York, and she looked both poised and confident.

"How dare you run from me?" the man said. It was bluster, but it sounded oddly weak.

Zoe eyed him with disdain. "There was no running involved, Father. I am a grown woman. My whereabouts are my own business."

"You've worried your mother sick."

Zoe didn't rise to the bait. She had told Liam about the phone calls between mother and daughter, and he knew she would never say anything to get her mother in trouble.

Zoe tucked her hands in the pockets of her skirt, perhaps so her father wouldn't see them shake. Liam knew her pretty well by now. Beneath her pretense of calm, she was very upset. "Why are you here, Father?"

"I want you to come home. I want you to join me in the business."

"You know that's not going to happen."

"So you're going to throw your life away? Is that what you want? To spend all your time flitting from one town to the next?"

Liam winced inwardly. Had Zoe seen Liam's opinions as mirrors of her father's disapproval?

She shook her head. "I enjoy my music and it makes people happy. What you do makes people want to kill themselves."

"Now you're being ridiculous."

"I don't think so. The last covert takeover you staged caused a very nice man to commit suicide."

"You don't understand the ins and outs of business." His voice was haughty and patronizing.

Liam stepped forward. "I think Zoe would like you to leave."

"And who the hell are you?"

"My name is Liam Kavanagh. I own the Silver Beeches. I won't let one of our guests be harassed."

"I'm taking my daughter home with me."

"No, you're not." Liam took a deep breath. "Even the worst of fathers wouldn't send his daughter to jail. She has the money, and she'll give it back, won't you Zoe?"

To his eternal astonishment, Zoe took a step closer to her father, as if to say clearly that Liam was not speaking for her.

Mr. Henshaw frowned. "What money?"

Zoe turned to Pierre who had been hovering nearby. "Would you please send someone to my room to retrieve my guitar? Everything else is still packed in my suitcase." She faced her father. "I *will* go home with you because my vehicle is in the repair shop. I want to see Mother and let her know I'm okay. But you must understand that if you want me to have any kind of relationship with you at all, you're going to have to find someone else to join you in the business. Is that clear?"

Liam watched as her father seemed to deflate. "You'll change your mind."

"No, Daddy. I won't. And if you ever lay a hand on me again, or Mother for that matter, I'll have *you* arrested."

Liam realized that he had just witnessed a tiny kitten grow into a lioness. Zoe had found the courage somewhere to face down her father, and like most bullies, her autocratic parent caved when confronted by real confidence.

"What's gotten into you?" Mr. Henshaw muttered. But it was a rhetorical question.

Liam took Zoe's arm. "I need to speak with you…privately." When she resisted, he was shocked. The irrepressible light of joy and happiness that lit her blue eyes from within was gone. "I won't let him involve the police, Zoe. You don't have to go with him."

She jerked free of his grasp. "I have no reason to stay here." Seven words. Seven flat, icy words.

"I don't understand. Doesn't your father want his money back?"

For a brief moment, a flame of anger and hurt broke through her mask of calm. Her lips trembled. "The money is mine, Liam. I inherited three million dollars from my grandmother when I turned eighteen."

Before he could come up with a response, a bellman returned with Zoe's luggage, and in minutes, she and her father were gone.

For his entire adult life up until this point, Liam had known exactly where to plot his course. He had a purpose and a mission. His job was to steer the Kavanagh fortunes and support his mother in the way his father never had.

In the wake of Zoe's departure, he was lost. He spent days floundering in a sea of confusion and guilt. When the pain of losing her became too much, he hiked the mountains, trying to outrun the knowledge that he had let her down. He had called her a thief and a liar. All in the guise of being supportive. No wonder she had left.

As the days passed, several things became clear. He was as fallible as the next human being. And his father had not been an evil man. Liam's dad had chased a dream with mortal consequences. He had betrayed his marriage vows. He had deserted his family. But his death was an accident. An awful, tragic accident.

One month to the day after Zoe walked out of his life, Liam stood in front of the Silver Beeches, keys in hand, ready to return Zoe's at-long-last-repaired van to her. It would be a lengthy road trip, but he had a feeling that he needed the time alone behind the wheel to prepare for what would most likely be a chilly reception.

His mother, who had urged him to take an extended leave of absence, came outside to bid him goodbye. She ran her hand along the side of the vintage VW van painted aqua and white with yellow daisies. "Take all the time you need, Liam. I want you to be happy. Your brothers are nearby if I need them. You're free, my dearest boy. God bless."

He hugged her, feeling a trace of guilt for leaving, but more importantly, exhilaration and hope for the road ahead. "Thank you, Mom. I love you."

"I love *you,* son. And if it's any comfort, I'd stake my life on the fact that Zoe loves you, too."

"I treated her badly." His lack of faith in the woman he claimed to love still scored him with guilt.

"We all make mistakes, Liam. She understands that. Sometimes a simple, sincere apology means the world."

"I hope you're right." The alternative didn't bear thinking about. "I'll keep you posted. Don't work too hard."

Maeve grinned, taking years off her age. "Work keeps me young. Now go. Get out of here. And don't come back until I have at least some hope of having grandchildren one day."

Zoe felt the sun warming her back as she knelt to pluck weeds from among the seedlings in her mother's well-tended flower bed. The Henshaws employed a full-time gardener, but this monotonous task was one Zoe enjoyed. She let her mind wander, hearing the birds sing around her and smelling the piquant odor of freshly turned earth.

She realized that she was more centered, more at peace than the young woman who had slipped away on Christmas Eve so many weeks ago. Loving Liam had taught her to look inside herself for the truth of her emotions.

She didn't hate her father, but they would likely never see eye to eye. Finally finding her backbone and dealing with him these last few weeks had not been easy, but Zoe's reward was the way her mother had blossomed. The older woman smiled now.

Beneath the familial triumphs, though, was the ever-present ache of losing Liam. She missed him terribly. Without even realizing it, she had come to regard Silver Glen as home, and the head of the Kavanagh clan as her heart's desire.

No matter how much she grieved, she knew she had been right to let him go. He still had doubts about her, perhaps because they were too different. In all fairness, some of the rift was her fault. She had kept too many secrets. She hadn't trusted him quickly enough, nor deeply enough. She was tempted to go back to North Carolina and apologize for that, if nothing else.

But she didn't want Liam to take her back for the wrong reasons. Though he'd said he loved her, she suspected that his declaration was the result of an overdeveloped sense of responsibility. She knew he *wanted* her. And perhaps he had convinced himself that what he felt was the real thing. The truth was, however, Liam took care of people. His mother, his family, the hotel… Zoe would be just another millstone around his neck.

She was in the zone, as they say, intent on her task, when two male feet appeared in her peripheral vision.

"Need a hand?"

The all-too-familiar voice sent a chill down her spine. She stood up slowly, wiping her fingers on the legs of her ancient, faded jeans. "Liam." It wasn't much of a response, but it was the only one she could come up with. Her heart leapt in joyful surprise, but her brain beat the girly response into submission. "What are you doing here?"

He looked so good it made her chest hurt. The only time she had seen him dressed so casually was the night she sang in Dylan's bar. Today he wore a dark blue knit shirt that matched his eyes. His hair was a trifle longer than usual, and he looked tired.

With hands in his pockets, he regarded her intently. "I brought your van back to you. It's parked out front."

"Ah. Well, thank you."

"I left Silver Glen a week ago and took my time getting up here. Toured Monticello. Caught a couple of museums in D.C. Saw the world's largest Coke can in a little town in Jersey. Slept in your van almost every night."

"I see." But she didn't. Not at all. Was he trying to tell her something? "How are you getting home?"

"I'm not going home. At least not yet."

"Okay." Still she was baffled.

His lips twisted. "I'm sorry I didn't believe you about the money."

She saw genuine regret on his face. "I overreacted, Liam. And I was partly to blame for your assumptions. It's hard for me to trust people. If I had told you the truth sooner, you never would have thought I was a criminal."

His theatrical wince made her smile.

"*Criminal* is a strong word. But tell me something, Zoe. Why *did* you carry all that cash?"

"That part is easy to explain. When my father and I first had our falling-out, not this past December, but earlier, I hit the road not wanting to be found. I knew if I used credit cards, he could trace me."

"But you used one to check in at Silver Beeches."

"True. So I guess a shrink would say I was tired of running."

"No comment." His smile was rueful. "Sorry I interrupted. Please continue."

"Anyway, the first time I left, I withdrew a large sum of money from my own account and hid it inside Bessie."

"Bessie?"

"That's what I call my van. I've traveled the world enough to know that a single woman needs to have a backup plan for emergencies."

"I hope you never have an emergency that big. Aren't you wondering if your money is intact?"

"Is it?"

"Of course." He ran both hands through his hair. "Gary thought I was insane when I asked him to paint the van. Again. To its original color."

"That was sweet of you."

"It seemed the least I could do."

Zoe shifted from one foot to the other. Perhaps she should ask him in for tea, but she wasn't at all sure why he had come, other than to return her vehicle. "Well, thanks again," she said brightly.

His gaze grew stormy. "I told you I loved you."

Like she needed reminding. "I know you did. But you're a fixer, Liam. A caretaker. You see people in trouble and you want to help. I seemed like a desperate case, so you convinced yourself that you loved me and needed to save me from myself. It was a heat-of-the-moment kind of thing. Very noble, but not legally binding."

"Do you care about me at all?"

His steady question set her feet in quicksand. The more she struggled, the faster she would sink. "Of course. I had a lot of fun with you."

"Fun." He said it like a curse.

"You seem to be getting upset. Perhaps you should go."

"Damn it, Zoe." Without warning, he yanked her close, his strong arms binding her to him as he kissed her senseless.

She might have gotten too much sun already. Her mother always warned her to wear a hat. When she could finally catch a breath, she pushed her hands against his chest. But it was like trying to move Mt. Rushmore. "You don't have to do this. I'm fine."

He glared at her. "Well, I'm not. You waltzed into my life and painted it all the colors of the rainbow. After you left, everything was gray again."

"You have a great life. Everything a man could want."

"No." He said it simply. "I don't have you, Zoe."

"You think I'm unfocused and lack ambition."

He nuzzled her nose with his as his hands stroked up and down her arms. "I think you're amazing, and just the person to plan our road trip."

"Our road trip?" His kisses must have fired a few synapses.

"I've taken a sixty-day sabbatical from the hotel. My mother sends her regards."

Zoe gaped. "But you love that hotel."

He shook his head, his eyes filled with happy tenderness. "I love *you*. And at the risk of sounding egocentric, I'd like to know how you feel about me. Am I too much of a stuffed shirt for a pretty gypsy with sunshine hair and a voice like an angel?"

Tears welled in her eyes. "I couldn't bear it if things didn't work out." She didn't want to get her hopes up. Walking away from him once had nearly destroyed her. And their relationship had been so complicated, it was hard to believe he loved who she really was.

"Then we'll take a trial run. In Bessie. On the open road. Wherever you like."

"Really?" It felt like Christmas and her birthday all rolled into one.

"Really. But I do have one condition."

"That sounds ominous." She patted his chest and rested her cheek over his heart.

"Look at me, sweetheart." He backed away and fished in his pocket, extracting a small, elegant box. "That day in New York when you were studying French impressionists at the museum, I sneaked away and bought this. I know you need time to think about marrying me, but I want you to wear it."

The ring was a flawless square-cut solitaire, at least two carats or more, surrounded by tiny sparkling stones. She barely breathed as he slid it onto the ring finger of her left hand. "Oh, Liam…"

He lifted her fingers to his lips and kissed them. "Please, Zoe."

"Please what?"

"You know what."

She stared down at her hand, tilting and twisting it so that the sun caught the facets of the diamonds and sent prisms of color in every direction. When she looked back at Liam, he had his arms crossed over his chest. His gaze was watchful.

Flinging herself into his arms, forcing him to catch her, she kissed him with every bit of the longing she had bottled up for the last few weeks. "Of *course* I love you, you big doofus. And if you ever get around to proposing, I'll say yes."

His eyebrows went up. "I thought I already did."

"You alluded to it. That's different."

He was breathing hard, his face flushed. "Marry me, Zoe. Create babies with me. Sing to our children. Make love with me in our bed. You've taught me how to stop and smell the roses. Let me share my big, boisterous family with you."

"Oh, Liam…"

"You already said that," he teased.

"My parents will probably want a big society wedding. I *am* their only child, you know."

"I can live with that. I just can't live without you."

He scooped her up in his arms and strode toward the front yard.

Zoe linked her arms around his neck. "Where are we going?"

"Bessie should be the first to know, don't you think?"

"Well, she *was* responsible for bringing me to Silver Glen."

"We're never getting rid of this van," he said fervently.

"Whatever you say, dear."

He dropped her on her feet and backed her up against the

door that concealed a huge chunk of cash. "Thank you," he said, his lips brushing the tender skin below her ear.

"For what?"

"For being you, Zoe. For being you...."

* * * * *

If you loved this first Kavanagh novel,
don't miss Dylan's story,
BABY FOR KEEPS
coming June 2014.
Only from USA TODAY bestselling author
Janice Maynard
and Harlequin Desire.

Don't miss Janice Maynard's first family saga,
THE MEN OF WOLFF MOUNTAIN!

INTO HIS PRIVATE DOMAIN
A TOUCH OF PERSUASION
IMPOSSIBLE TO RESIST
THE MAID'S DAUGHTER
ALL GROWN UP
TAMING THE LONE WOLFF
A WOLFF AT HEART

All available now from Harlequin Desire!

REQUEST YOUR FREE BOOKS!
2 FREE NOVELS PLUS 2 FREE GIFTS!

HARLEQUIN® Desire

ALWAYS POWERFUL, PASSIONATE AND PROVOCATIVE

YES! Please send me 2 FREE Harlequin Desire® novels and my 2 FREE gifts (gifts are worth about $10). After receiving them, if I don't wish to receive any more books, I can return the shipping statement marked "cancel." If I don't cancel, I will receive 6 brand-new novels every month and be billed just $4.55 per book in the U.S. or $4.99 per book in Canada. That's a savings of at least 13% off the cover price! It's quite a bargain! Shipping and handling is just 50¢ per book in the U.S. and 75¢ per book in Canada.* I understand that accepting the 2 free books and gifts places me under no obligation to buy anything. I can always return a shipment and cancel at any time. Even if I never buy another book, the two free books and gifts are mine to keep forever.

225/326 HDN F4ZN

Name	(PLEASE PRINT)

Address	Apt. #

City	State/Prov.	Zip/Postal Code

Signature (if under 18, a parent or guardian must sign)

Mail to the **Harlequin® Reader Service:**
IN U.S.A.: P.O. Box 1867, Buffalo, NY 14240-1867
IN CANADA: P.O. Box 609, Fort Erie, Ontario L2A 5X3

Want to try two free books from another line?
Call 1-800-873-8635 or visit www.ReaderService.com.

* Terms and prices subject to change without notice. Prices do not include applicable taxes. Sales tax applicable in N.Y. Canadian residents will be charged applicable taxes. Offer not valid in Quebec. This offer is limited to one order per household. Not valid for current subscribers to Harlequin Desire books. All orders subject to credit approval. Credit or debit balances in a customer's account(s) may be offset by any other outstanding balance owed by or to the customer. Please allow 4 to 6 weeks for delivery. Offer available while quantities last.

Your Privacy—The Harlequin® Reader Service is committed to protecting your privacy. Our Privacy Policy is available online at www.ReaderService.com or upon request from the Harlequin Reader Service.

We make a portion of our mailing list available to reputable third parties that offer products we believe may interest you. If you prefer that we not exchange your name with third parties, or if you wish to clarify or modify your communication preferences, please visit us at www.ReaderService.com/consumerchoice or write to us at Harlequin Reader Service Preference Service, P.O. Box 9062, Buffalo, NY 14269. Include your complete name and address.

HDDIR13R

She looked prettier than a painted picture come to life.
Yep. Trouble with a capital *T* if he didn't get his mind back
on business.

"After you learn the details of your share of the Lassiter
fortune, you'll be able to buy me dinner next time." *Next
time?* Man, he was getting way ahead of himself, and that
was totally out of character for his normally cautious self.

Hannah looked about as surprised as he felt over the
comment. "That all depends on if I actually agree to accept
my share, and that's doubtful."

He couldn't fathom anyone in their right mind turning
down that much money. But before he had a chance to toss
out an opinion, their waiter showed up with their entrées.

Logan ate his food with the gusto of a field hand, while
Hannah basically picked at hers, the same way she had with
the salad. By the time they were finished, and the plates were
cleared, he had half a mind to invite her into the nearby bar
to discuss business. But dark and cozy wouldn't help rein in
his libido.

Hannah tossed her napkin aside and folded her hands before her. "Okay, we've put this off long enough. Tell me the details."

Logan took a drink of water in an attempt to rid the dryness in his throat. "The funds are currently in an annuity. You have the option to leave it as is and take payments. Or you can claim the lump sum. Your choice."

"How much?" she said after a few moments.

He noticed she looked a little flushed and decided retiring to the bar might not be a bad idea after all. "Maybe we should go into the lounge so you can have a drink before I continue."

Frustration showed in her expression. "I don't need a drink."

He'd begun to think he might. "Just a glass of wine to take the edge off."

She leaned forward and nailed him with a glare. *"How much?"*

"Five million dollars."

"I believe I will have that drink now."

Don't miss
FROM SINGLE MOM TO SECRET HEIRESS
Available May 2014
Wherever Harlequin® Desire books are sold.

HARLEQUIN®

Desire

ALWAYS POWERFUL, PASSIONATE AND PROVOCATIVE.

THE SARANTOS BABY BARGAIN
Billionaires and Babies
by Olivia Gates

Now guardian to his orphaned niece, Andreas Sarantos
wants only the best for her, which means marrying the
baby's adoptive mother—his ex-wife. But their arrangement
becomes less than convenient when his passion for
Naomi reignites....

Look for THE SARANTOS BABY BARGAIN
in May 2014, from Harlequin Desire!
Wherever books and ebooks are sold.

Don't miss other scandalous titles from the
Billionaires and Babies miniseries,
available now wherever books and ebooks are sold.

HIS LOVER'S LITTLE SECRET
by Andrea Laurence

DOUBLE THE TROUBLE
by Maureen Child

YULETIDE BABY SURPRISE
by Catherine Mann

CLAIMING HIS OWN
by Elizabeth Gates

A BILLIONAIRE FOR CHRISTMAS
by Janice Maynard

THE NANNY'S SECRET
by Elizabeth Lane

SNOWBOUND WITH A BILLIONAIRE
by Jules Bennett

HD73314

Desire

ALWAYS POWERFUL, PASSIONATE AND PROVOCATIVE.

THE LAST COWBOY STANDING
Colorado Cattle Barons
by Barbara Dunlop

After a disastrous first meeting, Colorado rancher Travis and city gal Danielle don't expect to cross paths again. But when they end up in a Vegas hotel suite together, there's no denying the depths of their desires. Could she finally manage to lasso the last cowboy standing?

Look for THE LAST COWBOY STANDING
in May 2014 from Harlequin Desire!
Wherever books and ebooks are sold.

Don't miss other exciting titles from the
Colorado Cattle Barons miniseries by Barbara Dunlop,
available now wherever ebooks are sold.

A COWBOY'S TEMPTATION

MILLIONAIRE IN A STETSON

AN INTIMATE BARGAIN

A COWBOY IN MANHATTAN
A COWBOY COMES HOME

Colorado Cattle Barons: From the mountains to the boardroom, these men have everything under control—except their hearts.